PETERIO IGNITUS

PLANETARY

ANTHROPOLOGIST

Acknowledgements

I would like to thank Ken Roberts of the Ottawa Science Fiction Society for editing my manuscript and for delightful discussions.

I also thank Aaron, Stacey and Lucky from Advance Printers for the manuscript editing and layout.

TABLE OF CONTENTS

Chapter 1 - Different from Us

It is a sunny day and the bright colorful plot of huts shine amidst the shrubs in the meadow. The huts are small with thatched roofs made of twigs and plant stems, while the walls of the huts are branches of wood and straw entwined together. Hanging from the roofs over the windows are vines of flowers with colorful petals, red, purple and yellow. Food is everywhere as nuts, seeds, and fruit filled the baskets outside, and in the huts. It is a quiet day, as the inhabitants are beyond hunting for food. Suddenly, a boy rushes into a hut with a chair, which he places on the floor. He sits on it to test it, then moves it to a clearing on the floor. Taking out a brush made of straw, he starts to paint on the chair, a bright yellow star.

On a nearby hill are perched two men, both watching the boy through surveyor scopes. Peterio who has on him weapons and such gear, puts the scope back into his techie pack which is filled with computerized instruments. Born and bred on Earth, Peterio Ignitus is the lead anthropologist in the Committee of Planetary Anthropologists. Peterio is fair, with platinum blond hair and steel grey eyes. He is a youthful man with a sense for conversation and sport which belies the 550 years he lived. As chief anthropologist, he moves and talks faster than the others. "In order to lead my committee members", so he says. His specialty is the in-depth study of Homo sapiens sapiens who colonized on planets beyond Earth.

Beside him is his work associate, Andreus Saturne, who like Peterio is medium built for an Earthling, muscular and athletic at six feet. Both are tanned, and wearing specialized sunglasses which are equipped with radios. Over their heads, on hair that is bleached from the long exposures to the sun, they each are wearing protective caps. As safety gear they must wear outfits that are made of light weight material which can provide immunity against any danger from their environment. Andreus who is younger than Peterio, has also gained longevity in his 200 years of life.

Together, they work hundreds of million light years away from the Earth. They both studied the colonies of Humans who settled in the different galaxies, the Milky Way, and the Andromeda. As part of the Human Planetary Colonization Project which started in the 21st Century AD, mankind have ventured far from Earth. They both have not been back to Earth for decades.

Peterio and Andreus are scientists, well educated and multi-disciplined. Presently, they are in a study of some species of Genus Homo who were mysteriously found living in several planets in the Andromeda Galaxy. These Hominins are often referred to as the Archaic Humans. The two now make studies of the Homo sapiens neanderthalensis, and the Homo sapiens denisovan. Each species was found living in their own individual planets. In space now far from Earth, Andreus also encounters life forms, sometimes unimaginably different from species on Earth. In this kind of study of non-Earth forms, is where Andreus will have possibilities in a discovery of an intelligent alien species.

"Oh, I just thought they were different!" says Peterio. He turns his head to see that Andreus is crouched on the meadow plants a few feet away.

"Different from whom?" queries Andreus. He points his finger at himself and at Peterio.

Peterio wants to make a comparison, but not with themselves. He says *"Oh! Our usual planetary inhabitants out this way. They gave me a turn to get a peek over and again. But you know they appear to resemble the human* colonists at Copernicus and also at Adonis, our Earth originated aboriginal colonies at Galaxy Andromeda. The inhabitants in those planets were part of the colonization program and were teleported from those populations in Africa, and in South Pacific Islands, 400 years ago, in the 22nd Century AD. They are hunter gatherers who maintain their lifestyles, living in the jungles. They live very primitively " Peterio, waving his hands in gesture, added "Oh! But what do we have here?"

"The meadows here, all dispersed among patches of shrubs are eye-catching with all these flowers. Indeed, the inhabitants have been resourceful in using these plants and trees to build their huts. It's so beautiful here with the lakes and some mountains further away. There seem to be patches of water or oceans everywhere. It is always warm, with a little misty fog and rain, all year round. Throughout the different geological ages, the Earth had changing climate systems. Well, the climate system here now, on this planet, seems to be supportive of life. You know what is really interesting? It is that, by happenstance we discovered another intelligent life form in a life supporting system here! Another Gaia environment?" adds Andreus.

"We've been here long enough to see, that these are the only inhabitants scattered about in small groups. What really is important to us, is that this planet is not one of our colonist planets. *They are not even on any of our interplanetary routes. This is a wild shot, but could this group be another ancestral population from Earth transported here by the Force!"* Peterio laughs about what Force may have done. *"The theories for the spreading of the species of the Genus Homo throughout Earth, has its origins "From Africa once or several times into Europe or Asia at least 200-800,000 years ago" and "from Asia spreading throughout into North America as recent as 15,000 years ago. It is really fantastic, but have we another species of the Homo genus all the way here to these planets too!"*

Laughing Andreus says, *"With all the DNA studies done on fossils, it still is shaky ground to stand on when telling the story of the evolution of Genus Homo. Our discoveries of other species of the Genus Homo located out in the Andromeda Galaxy have revealed evidence for the spreading beyond Earth of the Hominins. Finding that out, was a real breakthrough! We were able to get some samples for DNA analysis to compare with the DNA from the fossils found on Earth! We never could have got to that vantage point, except for the work of the Force. That led to the debate on Earth about Force that you attended, and definitely on these colonies of the Archaic Humans. Force identified these Archaic Humans that He transported to those planets in the Galaxy Andromeda (M31). Here at Triangulum (M33), this race may not be aboriginals from a contemporary time living primitively. Maybe, as you pointed out, this race is another ancestral* species of the Genus Homo (Archaic Humans) that Force transported?"

Peterio switches on his computer, keying in a few orders. The screen flashes on 16 squares, each exhibiting different scenes of what appears to look like Humans in differing habitats. He declares "*This group is non-Human! It woke me up on a few things! I'll flash you through the screens. They were in the desert living on the sand, hunting the desert birds living on the desert plants. This screen shows you that they were on a beach, fishing with poles. They lived near the water amongst shrubs, making shelter amongst rocks and trees. Here, this screen reveals them in the mountains, hunting small animals in the caves where they lived. They were in different habitats all over the planet.*"

"*Why did they move around?*" asks Andreus pointing a finger at the pictures.

Exclaims Peterio, "*The scenes were from the first 300 years of my studies. These are different populations I studied on that planet. Being nomadic they would eventually find a niche in any of the many habitats. They were simple and not sophisticated enough to build structures; but had survived in each new habitat. They lived and died as such, in the wild. They had kept no records. In differing habitats where they* moved into, they changed little, only adopting a few new skills for hunting. From far away, when walking on two legs, they may look to be Human. But just examine these pictures closely! They each have four eyes in the head, two in the front and two on the sides. They can endure in the ruggedness of the landscapes and climb better than most of the Humans. The eyes and muscular legs were probably adaptations for their nomadic ways." exclaims Peterio excitedly.

"Did you think they were an intelligent species? Did you try to communicate with them? enquires Andreus.

"No!" answers Peterio. "They were more like the nomadic animals on Earth. Except they were involved in some kind of communication with each other. They just took what they needed to live on. The necessities for life."

"Oh! I see your point! So different from what I would have expected." says Andreus. "Back to the inhabitants here! They appear to be like Sapiens. Are you saying we can't be sure until we have proof of the fact? They are beautifying the buildings and making complexities out of simple things, for aesthetic reasons! However, it's is no breakthrough scientifically in making this comparison as evidence for an identification, "Sapiens". But I often love thinking of our species, for what they have done with the word "beautify." Andreus sparkles with enthusiasm as he now tries to make a case for Homo sapiens sapiens, instead of for the Archaic Humans.

"And they are self protective too!" adds Peterio.

"Oh" with a puzzled look from Andreus. *"Did you have a confrontation?"*

"I went to grab a basket of seeds from one of the boys. The mother came up to me and took it back. She shouted at me and waved a stick to send me away. Later she talked about me to her family while they sat together to eat. Waving her hand with an imaginary stick, she pointed at the boy. While they ate, they are speaking about their day. They were joyful, not revealing any alarm that some of them met up with us. It seemed not an unusual action for her to just scare me off. Although I was in full gear, she reacted as though I am just another creature who wandered into her territory. Territorial rights, she was protecting!" Peterio indicates this observation to Andreus.

Continuing on in the topic of human characteristics, Peterio introspects on human nature, *"Humans went on beautifying the Earth, with architecture, jewels, paintings, sculptures, spacious parks and luscious colorful gardens, and now designs that are geometrically precise in the technology of space stations and space vehicles. My little girl took interest in baking and decorating a cake before she learned how to send a scientific communique to my inter-computer. These days their interests in technological advancements in mathematics and science is only rivaled by these kinds of signifying human qualities. These ones are like us. But on our furthest reach out this way, when we saw some of our colonists, no one informed us about this colony. This is a discovery, novel and unique too! Especially if Force sent them here. Why are there human species brought out here so far from Earth?*

They are now here in Triangulum (M33). When is the next question? Unfortunately, these ones do not speak any of our languages to tell us anything!"

"You are right! There are no tools nor gadgets made of metal. They use rocks, trees and grasses. They are still primitive. Would they be on the road to become civilized?" says Andreus.

"We can inspect the rocks and soil to see what we have here." says Peterio who is searching for a task to do to get more ideas about them.

"Why don't we help them?" asks Andreus.

"They have made no metal tools. As I suspect they haven't discovered how to forge metal on fire!" adds Peterio. "Well. *They have fire. That's a start! And flint arrowheads. The boy is drawing with dye on wood. Have we a parallel comparison to the primitive cave drawings, or to the wall drawings at the dawn of Human civilization or to cuneiform language? That was proof of development in the communication of Modern Sapiens."*

"We must study more! And we can help them move along!" answers Andreus.

"Move ahead! Ugh! What will be their future if we do, or do not, intervene? It will be a peculiar kind of meeting! They are primitive and to meet with us, the space age? Extraordinary!" wonders Peterio.

"Let us sleep on it!" answers Andreus. Peterio and Andreus prepares a sheltered spot amongst the rocks and shrubs to sleep overnight. Their usual stayover is in their space vehicle but the outdoors seems safe and inviting this night. Both are wearing one-piece jumpsuits made of liquid repellent, light materials. Wrapped into their sleeping bags and pods, they both slept under the stars this night, outdoors. They remain far from where the inhabitants are, and kept close to the space vehicle, with all their gear.

14

The next day, Peterio checking his computer for the file on languages used on the Earth, says "*I found it! Their language resembles that of the early Modern Sapiens. Initially we have no evidence that language had existed for any of the Early Humans. In the caves, where their bones were found, were painted pictures on the walls. I initiated, the Force to arrange for the human explorers during the 24th Century AD, a teleportation to the days when the ancestral populations lived on Earth. Studies into the past were then possible. After the Neanderthals had started to disappear from the Earth and the Sapiens were increasing in numbers, the Sapiens' attempt to communicate, was rudimentary like this. We have some recordings from the visits. I can defend the hypothesis that the Force may have transported prehistoric Sapiens to this planet. This planet is in an extremely remote region, far from the other Human colonies in Milky Way or in Andromeda. The settlements of the other Homo species, the Archaic Humans established by Force in Andromeda, are near planets where our space explorers suggested for colonization of our Space Age Humans.*"

Andreus agrees "*This discovery, although in a remote region far from the others, would be of extreme importance if this be a colony of our Homo sapiens sapiens*".

"For now, I'll see if we can meet them and get some samples to do a genetics. Some cheek swabs and some blood samples. To test our hypothesis! I can't be more excited! Working with Force on the colonist teleportations is magnificent by far! But to have surprise colonies to make identifications of! It's just wonderful!" adds Peterio eager to work on their new discovery.

As the two talk, a group of the inhabitants comes up to the hill and confronts them. They look each other in the eyes. Not trusting Peterio amidst all his instruments, they start to throw stones at him and Andreus. Peterio offers a *"Who are you? We are your friends! "* and makes a hand signal.

Both men grab their equipment, retreating from stones that are thrown at them; and run off as fast as they can. The group of planetarians pick up more stones from the ground, aiming at their fleeing targets. They chase Peterio and Andreus through the meadow and over the hill. As they suddenly see the space vehicle that Peterio and Andreus are heading for, they stop. They can see the two visitors disappear into the space vehicle. Peterio and Andreus leave the planet quickly, for the spaceship stationed out in space not too far away.

Remaining on the hill, the few startled, bewildered men become more than troubled, having seen a shiny flying object carry off their visitors. They point to some birds flying around and talk nervously about the two men and the vehicle that can fly off and disappear from view. Not ever witnessing such an event they laughed; but just talking one over the other, they came to no conclusion about what to do. Having spent much time on the hill, in order to see if the flying object will appear again; they decided that it will not come back. They went to look at the meadow where the vehicle was and then quickly left to tell the others in the community huts.

Peterio and Andreus know how excited all the anthropologists would be, after informing them that an ancient race of Humans may dwell on that planet they are orbiting. The anthropologists are all in agreement to make a study of this discovery. Also, they plan to establish a kinship with these planetarians. Peterio who felt the need for further investigation suggests again *"Could the possibility, be that these planetarians be members of the Archaic Humans, Homo sapiens neanderthalensis or Homo sapiens denisovan, or of the early Modern Humans, Homo sapiens sapiens. They have a form of language communication, that can assign the identification to be Sapiens. "*

Peterio and Andreus both laugh at the fact that their goals out here in space was the in-depth study of the colonists and other possible non-Earth species. They are both surprised that they definitely will be studying the Genus Homo again. Both grin at the idea that they would be looking at the whole picture, reviewing their own anthropological work done back on Earth.

A year passes by. Peterio and Andreus established a simplified form of communication with these natives. Their goal is to have all finally converse in English. This was decided to be the most applicable language, as visitors from the space station can also participate with the planetarians during their visits. When the discovery was made known, it was decided to orbit a space station around this planet.

Having made a contact with the locals of this planet, Peterio and Andreus look forward to joining in with their life activities, which are those of ancient days. They help their new men friends with their hunting, using spears they learned how to make. Also, with the women, they were involved with picking of fruit, and digging of some tuberous plants. The two then joined in for conversation and food around the cooking fire. It appeared to Peterio that their learning of the fire to keep warm and for the use in cooking food, may have been from when they were back on Earth. They took skills which spread around from group to group back on Earth, here to this planet. Peterio wondered if there would be a day when in conversation these people would be able to tell him of any knowledge of their origins on the Earth.

"Alas" says Peterio to Andreus one day, *"These inhabitants of the planet have befriended us, unusual visitors who arrive here through the skies."* When Peterio fell off a ledge on a rock cliff, scraping the skin off his leg and breaking a bone, several of the men helped lift him back to the huts. They were curious and wanted to watch the administering of space age medicine. To welcome the two visitors to the group, they built a hut to house them.

Eventually, the two visitors are able to collect samples for the DNA analysis. Their study can be verified scientifically, now. As the two stayed on, in their visit, they want to have some experience in the ancient lifestyles. This opportunity for study with primitive Sapiens from Earth will not be lost. All information gathered for study by the two are subsequently, sent back to the space station for further analyses by the scientific crew here. Some of the other anthropologists have descended from the space station to find their own way around the planet; and definitely to make a personal acquaintance with the planetarians as Peterio and Andreus did.

One morning, the geneticist Evala Struvante makes her way from the Space Station and heads into the forests. Evala, a medium built brunette is one of the many female crew in the Space Station. As a scientist, Evala spends her days on her laboratory analyses, in her own cubicle at the Space Station Laboratory. The laboratory is huge and full of scientific equipment, and lots of staff running around in their laboratory garments. On other days when her work can wait, she goes out for strenuous work outs at the Space Station Gymnasium. But she loves the planet more, and makes an excuse to get out of the Space Station as often as she could. Evala was born on Trek21 but also studied on Earth. At 80 years old, Evala has gained superhuman status, for her involvement in space-time travelling. Younger than most of the crew, Evala feels freer to escape the routine of her scientific work and travel out to explore the planet on her own. Today, Peterio is hunting for some game for the supper he is going to share with these hunter gatherers, when she went out looking for him.

"*Peterio!*" screams Evala through the bushes, as she sees him poised to make a throw with his spear. She interrupts his hunt but she is bringing news!

"*Evala, what are you doing here?*" cries out Peterio, turning his head around to see if anyone else is there.

Evala talks quickly and joyfully, saying "*They are one of us!*"

Peterio enquiring as he walks towards her, "*You mean the DNA is done and that we have a classification for these people, now! Sapiens?*"

Evala, as she throws her hands in the air, makes her claim to Peterio, "*Yes, I got the analysis up in the station and they are Sapiens! We need to know how old this population is? Further analysis with the DNA, I suppose. However, I wonder if we can measure for different kinds of isotopes? Some heavy isotopes, or maybe the radioactive isotopes. Oh! But they are alive. Although we can't make any exclusions, they could have some old material in them.*" She starts to laugh now making a comment on what she knows isn't possible. "*Is there such a thing as time warp on isotope decay? We can consider the extraordinary here! Something for the others to think about! Or ask the Force one day! Ha Ha Ha.*"

Peterio grabs the scientist, and swings her around. They both jump up and down, laughing. This is what they all wanted. Both shouted "*Hurrah*" for their new find! Peterio suggests, "*Somehow they appear primitive and ancient!*"

Evala agrees and declares that " *They have no knowledge of our technology.*"

Peterio wagers, "*I'll bet on 20,000 years ago for their age.*"

Evala complies to the wager and says, "*I 'll bet younger than that!*" Evala is excited now to go back to her analyses to look for more answers.

Peterio replies. "*The winner gets to eat dinner made by the other!*"

Evala agrees to the suggestion again. "*You got the bet! I'm going to look for Andreus now, and he will be happy to know. He's been spending a lot of time teaching them more phrases for communication. I'll head back to the huts.* "

Peterio and Andreus joins the space crew for a celebration in the Space Station. A few days later, while Peterio and Andreus heads back to the planet to join in for the group hunt, the crew aboard the Space Station is still buzzing about Evala's conclusive evidence. Out further from the huts, the two discover that some other groups from nearby, have wandered into the hunt territory. Although, these hunters seem not to be adversive to one another. Sometimes they talk to one another but eventually after meeting, they separate again.

Peterio suggests *"It appears that there may be lots of groups here. They may be another population of the same race. But they choose to band together in smaller groups. It makes sense, for the purpose of getting food and preserving orderliness, smaller groups would be better. In the theory, the size of the population or group corresponds directly with the size of brain development. Smaller groups make sense for the primitives!"*

"Why don't we travel out beyond and correspond with these other groups." suggests Andreus. *"We are doing well now, as we have a common language to make use of!"*

*   *   *   *   *

Over several decades, all the inhabitants on the planet have met up with, in friendly encounters, with Peterio and his cohorts. Peterio also began spending much of his time enriching the lives of these Ancient Humans. He wanted to give them more than just the learning of a language for their communication.

"Peterio are you sure they are good now, so we can leave them?" Andreus asks sadly as he knows that the time spent here is coming to an end.

"Yes! Over the years we've been coming here they learned new skills. How to forge metallic elements to make alloys of metals. They now have utensils, boats and wagons that can be pulled by animals. We encouraged them to build villages and roads to connect them. But without the knowledge on how to make machinery like those made on Earth during the Industrial Revolution, or during the Age of Inventions; they are still not technological and remain rural villagers with a farming lifestyle."

Andreus interrupts and says, "Can they without our help, develop the machinery and tools?"

"While they are still small in population numbers and not involved in anything intellectual, I do not think it is probable that any kind of genius such as Isaac Newton will arise from this population, at present. Anyhow, we are not going to be abrupt and suddenly help them! Let us see what will happen, firstly! " suggests Peterio.

"Force acknowledged that He sent Sapiens to live on this planet! However, we did not get a full picture of what Force is doing yet." suggests Andreus. Both Peterio, Andreus and the remaining scientists at the space station, are bewildered for the aim or purpose of the colonization efforts of Force. Continues Andreus, "Why move the Archaics of the Genus Homo away from Earth? And why move an Ancient race of Sapiens far from all other Sapiens, whether Archaic, Primitive or Space Age?"

Peterio continues to add to Andreus' remarks, "I sent word so that there will not be any immigration here by any of the colonists. We will send envoys to keep in touch. They are to be left a population pure from other colonists. When the DNA was thoroughly repeated by those at the colonies, we have definitely verification of early Homo sapiens sapiens. They were sent here by Force as you say, when Humans were at the dawn of civilization. Aside, just to let you know, at the last Earth debate, we were informed by Force, of His colonization into different planets, the Archaic Humans. He identified all the ones He had relocated into these faraway planets. On Earth, they were Neanderthals, Denisovans, Heidelbergensis, and Erectus. Back there, Neanderthals had diversified from Sapiens 500,000 years ago. But their fossils were found together in some caves in Spain and France aged 40,000 years old. Denisovan fossils were found in the Siberian deserts as recent as 15 - 30,000 years ago. The

25

hypothesis is that the Neanderthals and the Denisovans may have married or have been killed by Modern Sapiens in what is now Europe or Asia. There remains no evidence of these species on the Earth since those days. As you also know! When we completed the study for these newly discovered Archaic Humans, a brand-new picture will open up again for the theory of evolution of the Human race. "

"These theories always fascinated me! We can make further contributions to ongoing hypotheses. The Archaic Human colonies are in the Galaxy Andromeda where Space Age Human colonies are. In Triangulum, we only met up with this population of prehistoric Sapiens from Earth and some non-Earth species, who all are planet bound. Definitely we are impressed with Force, to have navigated us here!" remarks an inquisitive, enthusiastic Andreus.

"We will bring back this news to Earth. Later, debates which will be scheduled on Earth for these new discoveries, will include comments from Force!" says Peterio.

Andreus takes a breath, as he has all this new knowledge to talk about. *"The Denisovans learned to be sophisticated from our Human intervention on Planet Denisovana, of the Galaxy Andromeda. The Neanderthals without our interventions are making great strides in their development also."*

Peterio makes a remark on these planetarians. *"These Humans on this planet have not evolved beyond being hunter gatherers when we met. With help from us they developed into village farmers. We can check up in stages for any signs that may be telltale of any further development. Like using a peering telescope, we will look upon them for their "evo-devo."*

"And easily done, as I worked out a system where they can send messages to us. " Andreus says of his successful involvement to help in communications.

Peterio reminds him *"Don't imagine that our naming the planet Galileo is not appropriate! It 's like having a telescopic view of them from our distant, space age point of view. Earthlings went to Space Age very fast after the Age of Inventions, in the 20th Century AD. Although, there were groups who were more or less rural farmers. They remained like that for centuries on Earth, and they lived amongst those who were technologically advanced. They also made the same preferences as they became colonists on these planets out here."*

"Yes, on the Earth back then, some fought not to be techie. Not interested in technology nor space faring. We visited such colonists at Planet Drake31. A lot of them teleported to

these planets during the 23rd Century AD but choose to remain in their simple lifestyles whether on Earth or beyond." says Andreus. *"And there is no denial that they are civilized and intelligent."*

"We will see how these humans, here at Galileo will change." Peterio and Andreus together agree. *"Yes, these inhabitants will be named Galileans, on their Planet, Galileo. This honours the famous Galileo, an Earthling who lived in the 1600 AD and who invented the telescope".*

Peterio happily says, *"These are the first Sapiens whom Force had taken away from Earth, further to the colonization efforts in our space programs. Later I expect to find more species of the Genus Homo here or beyond. Then also to study our colonists out here. I need to map a chronology of the work of Force and of our pioneer space exploration and colonization missions out here. All the colonists are volunteers who emigrated from Earth to live a pioneering life in other planets of the Universe. They come from all walks of life.* "Peterio says of the pioneers who he was proud of. *"And these planets are amongst the exoplanets discovered by Earth-made telescopes since the 21st Century."*

So, it is decided by the Committee of Planetary Anthropologists that Peterio and Andreus will now leave this Galaxy Triangulum (M33) with their news, shocking and enigmatic, but intriguing. The space vehicle was started, and Peterio and Andreus depart from Galileo and head for the Space Station orbiting this planet. The others of the Committee in the Space Station will stay in touch with the Galileans. Peterio and Andreus will head homeward to Milky Way, for Earth.

The scientists remaining in the Space Station will conduct their scientific work as usual, during the years ahead without Peterio and Andreus. All the Galileans felt sad to see them leave this planet. The Galileans will continue with their newly learned skills. That evening the sun set and the villages turn down their lights in Galileo. As the darkness abounds, the aromas of sweet floral scents drift in the wind. A few birds chirp while the larger animals outside murmur, as they also lie down for their sleep. Peterio and his crew travelled out into the deep darkness of space. The crew took a good look at all the stars and gases, which radiated a beautiful display of bright colours outside the wide window of their space vehicle. They will meet up with the space ship that is nearby and continue their journey to Andromeda and then on to the Milky Way. Peterio and the engine crew will arrange for the engine computer to auto pilot the space ship, for the years ahead going home. The Human crew will be in hibernation.

Chapter 2 - The Interplanetary Visits

Alfred Mendel works with Denisovans who live at Planet Denisovana in the Galaxy Andromeda. Alfred is a Homo sapiens sapiens and he was delighted when the prestigious Committee of Planetary Anthropologists sent him to Denisovana to work. He heard Force had transported the Denisovans there, over 100,000 years ago. Denisovans remaining on Earth were eventually replaced by Sapiens 15-30,000 years ago.

Peterio and Alfred together founded the project to initiate interplanetary travels between planets where the Archaic Humans dwell and those where the Colonists live, at Andromeda. Hence, the blueprint for the mapping of all interplanetary routes was begun by Peterio in cooperation and collaboration with Force. Much later, as Peterio had to leave, the project was carried on by Alfred. It was at that time when Peterio was initially sent with a new work colleague, who is Andreus to explore the further reaches of these colonies, and outwards for the first visits into the galaxy Triangulum (M33). Alfred was not alone on the project, as Peterio can always make a visit, and as a few of the Denisovans who were Peterio's students were trained to help him.

* * * * *

The people on the flight to Denisovana from the planets in the region, are walking down the stairs, and stepping off the space jet onto the landing. Alfred who takes a holiday to the other planets in this Galaxy every few years, appears not to be among them. His Denisovan work associate and friend, Tedrid, becomes alarmed. *"Where's Alfred Mendel? This is a homecoming as he has been away for 2 years. I have a previous communique sent to me from Alfred that he will be on this flight."* Tedrid says to his assistants who accompanied him to the Denisovana Space Centre.

The official who brought back the bad news says, on seeing Tedrid. *"Alfred had died just before the return flight from Trek3 was to leave. Through an accident, his vehicle ditched and burst into flames. Alfred's body will be returned to his home, on one of the colonist planets or back to Earth where he was born."*

Tedrid breaks down and cries when they told him. This is awful news that he has to bring back to the Denisovans, who all loved Alfred. Tedrid who is forty years old in Earth years, had made friends with Alfred during his lengthy apprenticeship on the Project. He now has to, as does the official, report to Peterio, the

31

death of Alfred Mendel; and that a reorganization of the work that Alfred, Tedrid and Peterio were involved in, is now needed.

Months later, the Denisovans lead by Tedrid were tidying Alfred's filing cabinet, when Tedrid found some interesting paperwork. Tedrid has in his hands the log left by Alfred. He reads it.

Tedrid was very impressed by what Alfred wrote in his report on "Project: Denisovana and Interplanetary Travels". (Founded by Peterio Ignitus, Alfred Mendel, Force at Denisovana, Andromeda). "*At Planet Denisovana, I communicated with the Denisovans in their language which I picked up easily. 100,000 years of "evo-devo" and they are sophisticated, different from their ancient form, whose Human counterpart my ancestor, was the caveman. On Earth, this species Denisovan, may have married the modern Sapiens. At Andromeda, these two species meet again. Only here, the possibility exists of a union between Denisovan, who is now modern with technology, and Sapiens who is Space Age. Denisovans are both physically strong, and very athletic. Being carnivorous they feed on ungulates brought from Earth. They also feed on other animals and some plants and berries, local to this planet. In addition to the hunter-gatherer lifestyle, they developed the aptitude to became diligent farmers, breeding animals and* *food crops. I taught technology to deliver them to Space Age. It is education to the level, sophisticated enough for them to work with us. Sapiens, took 300 years to learn what I initiate for them to learn. I've spent 60 years at Denisovana dedicated to this purpose that Denisovans can have an education. This is one of my biggest efforts. I am presently working with a Denisovan, Tedrid Brown Armstrong. I gave him the name "Armstrong" after the first man who with his crew of the NASA APOLLO 11 mission, landed and walked on the moon of Earth, 20th Century AD. Tedrid is inspired by these space travels. The Denisovans are learning English and they often stop by our study office to practice communication with Tedrid and myself, in English.*

Visitors from the other planets include the Colonists. They started influencing the Denisovans to initiate an interest for interplanetary travelling. In so much as to desire settling in other planets. I plan for the Denisovans, a schedule of much interplanetary exploration. Human colonists come to these planets in the space exploration efforts and then to settle in Andromeda as they did in Milky Way Galaxy. These Archaic Humans, species of Genus Homo are their planetary neighbours, in Andromeda. They were sent here, by Force. On Earth, the fossil record is scant. In the 20-21st Century AD scientists using the fossils they discovered, presented a timeline for the existence on a geological scale, members of Genus Homo. The very collection of the fossils of these species *of this Genus attributes to evidence of their life on Earth. That defined Homo sapiens sapiens to be modern Human, and other more primitive species of the Genus Homo, the Archaic Human. DNA data on the fossils has matched with DNA from these planetarians.*

I am meticulous in keeping records of the Denisovans in Andromeda. These records are of extant species! Peterio Ignitus, had earlier informed all the anthropologists, that a teleported trip back into specific times in the geological past of Earth, would enable a look at these species as they were alive on Earth. Without of course, disruption to the actual historical events. A visit to that prehistoric time would be a visit with these peoples, when they would be at the very primitive level. Different from who they are now. On these planets of Andromeda, we encountered both Denisovans and Neanderthals. Both are civilized and moving ahead as did the Sapiens on Earth."

Aside, there are also other travellers from other planets who visited Denisovana. Alien travellers, not of Earth origins. The hope for all at Denisovana and their neighbouring planets, is that these visits be friendly. So far so good, as no battles took over friendly visits. I have recorded videos of the visits. I keep records of all visits of outgoing and incoming explorers to this region in the Andromeda galaxy. The records are also complete with calculations. Peterio and I are the researchers who founded the mapping project with Force. If I had the time, I would teach all my assistants the necessary computations in the records of the mapping and chronology of the interplanetary travels. To date, Tedrid Brown Armstrong, Ian Mendel, Peterio Ignitus and myself are the only ones who have knowledge of the records. I have had no time either to explain to all the Earthlings who may have travelled here. They are busy, involved in their own missions.

Alfred Mendel, 50/27/26th Century AD, Planet Denisovana, Andromeda Galaxy

Tedrid schedules for the work to continue by himself and some Denisovan assistants. These Denisovans resembled Alfred, in having fair skin and dark hair. But Alfred, being taller at a height greater than 6 feet, had towered over the slightly built Denisovans. To learn more of the science that these Humans brought to Denisovana, these assistants often needed advice from Alfred. Alfred whom they often are found hovered around, gave illusions that the bigger Humans from afar have stature extraordinaire with these natives of Denisovana. Especially when these Humans have so many suggestions and knowledgeable information! But between these two species who can work together, it was with more than respect that each had for one another. Tedrid who is in a very unique role, has the purpose now of providing them, the scientific expertise that he learned from Alfred. It is because of Tedrid's interest to learn from the space oriented Humans that will allow for the work to be continued. The Denisovans cannot be more than excited for him. He says at one of the meetings to his assistants, *"In recognition of all the work, that Alfred Mendel did for the "Project: Denisovana and Interplanetary Travels", we will have a Denisovan Study Centre built for the work he devoted so much time and effort, and we will honour this great Human, Alfred Mendel who was more than a friend to us. "*

Peterio, during the time he was studying the Sapiens at Galileo, was invited by Tedrid for the inaugural opening of the Denisovan Study Centre. He departed the planet in the Galaxy Triangulum, for Denisovana which is millions of light years away in the Galaxy Andromeda. He will also later, visit some of the colonists planets there and return with some gadgets for the Galileans.

At the opening of the Study Centre, all the invited guests are excited again for the work Tedrid will be carrying out. Peterio, although he is working on a project that he is very attached to, is more than honoured to be at this inauguration of the Centre; having taken another leave from his work. When

36

Peterio announces the opening of the Study Centre to the crowd of Denisovan and Sapiens scientists, and other colonists from the surrounding planets, all cheered for his leadership. *"More travellers will come to Denisovana. They will come to the Study Centre, and they will see all travels throughout this Galaxy displayed in maps, work that Alfred Mendel has started here. In honour of this friend of the Denisovans, we will continue the work of the mapping and chronologies of the interplanetary visits here in Andromeda. Tedrid Brown Armstrong, your very own Denisovan scientist who is both intellectual and capable, will have the role as director of the projects here."*

Tedrid goes to shake hands with Peterio and says, *"In my heart, Alfred who was my teacher, will remain my friend. It is a very special moment for me and all Denisovans! I will continue in his footsteps, as director of the project and with much joy!"*

All cheer for, the new Centre, the introduction of new staff, and a synopsis of the studies to be carried out, which was elaborated on by Tedrid. Numerous guests wander over to the tables for some Denisovan food. It is a celebration unique for Denisovans, as they are being honoured by the planetary community, especially Tedrid as a leading scientist. For the others, Sapiens, and a few other species of the Genus Homo, it is a new kind of meet and greet with each other. This event was an honoured activity as most of the guests were not familiar with the study of space science or science at all. When Alfred had befriended the Denisovans, he concentrated on the basic levels of education and communication, and had only educated a few of the Denisovans for the work in which he was involved. Music from Earth is piped over the speaker system, in memory of Alfred Mendel.

Tedrid works on the project without Alfred, but sometimes he feels lost. Over the years, Tedrid worked on a simpler project for the mapping and chronology of the interplanetary travels in the vicinity of Denisovana of the Andromeda Galaxy. *"Time warps, wormholes, collapse of space-time coordinates in the fabric of the space-time continuum, and entanglements were much of a difficulty for us. Without Alfred, it is a challenge for us. For all the calculations on the collected data, we did as much as we could."* as Tedrid reports to Peterio, who often went to Denisovana to help him with the work. Peterio had initiated calculations based on a cooperation with Force. He wants more time to work with Tedrid and his Denisovan assistants, but his other work, sent him to explorations far away in Triangulum.

It is somewhat of a miracle when Ian Mendel, a Human explorer, appears at the Centre. A few Humans live on this planet; and Tedrid who really enjoys the company of Humans, is very enthusiastic for this visit. Ian shows a preferred interest in the mapping project, and so Tedrid starts him as his assistant.

"The idea for the mapping of the Denisovan explorations, was originated by Peterio Ignitus and his student, Alfred Mendel. It never became research work for other Humans here, as they take on other tasks. No Humans around here understand it except for them! " Tedrid says to Ian. *"And you look somewhat like Alfred. Drop a few years to his aging and he can be you. Alfred likes to sport a nice cut to his hair adding a spike at top! While you have all this flowing hair! When you exchanged your travel garb for the laboratory coats, you look so like Alfred! Who are you? Are you some distant relative of Alfred's?"*

"Just the opposite! I was Alfred and Alfred was me, the same person. On one of the visits to Olympus, Milky Way Galaxy, the Force split Alfred, to be two clones, or as you might say, identical twins. Twins not separated at the embryo, in the cellular stage. But for us, at 250 years old. We both agreed not to stay in touch. I left Olympus, but never really showed up here at Denisovana. I knew not of his death, when I decided to visit Denisovana. As a Human I have a telepathic

sense. I knew, a problem was troubling Alfred. At that time, I was exploring Andromeda Galaxy and the neighbouring Galaxies. But I long to find the reason for this split! The project is important, but it belongs to Alfred. I, on the other hand, was just doing whatever I pleased. To my surprise, I am working on the project, myself now. But why did Alfred have to die? He would have reached 300 years old. It could have worked out also, that there were two of us. I am troubled that I am here and he is absent."

Tedrid becomes emotionally upset and surprised at hearing this and says, *"Thank you, for coming here and getting involved in the project. Alfred is gone now and it is rather astonishing to me that he never told me about you! Were you ever aware of the disaster, that took the life of your twin?"*

"No" says Ian. *"There are clones who keep the mental contact with each other by telepathic means. Synchrony. But we never!"*

"Where did you live? When did you become his twin? For decades, we carried out the explorations, together. Indeed, I never thought I would see again, the kind of dedication and excitement that Alfred puts into his work. You are like him." suggests Tedrid.

"Alfred was split into two, many decades ago. Although I never did any work on the project, I know about it, as it was started before he was split. I have all the same memory of the life activities of Alfred before the split. The project was kept going by you for numerous years and I can see that there are some very important data, you collected on your own. This mapping in Galaxy Andromeda is a showcase for further studies into interplanetary visits. During the years after I left him, Alfred would continue to make the mappings until the death as you told me. It really has to be calculated from his mathematical genius level. Peterio Ignitus initiated the mapping with Force and was the only one with all the knowledge! I only can work from the initial knowledge we had together, but with a study of his calculations I will be able to take it on. And with your guidance, Tedrid, and with the expertise of Peterio when we can get him, we will be able to work out the calculations in the mapping of the interplanetary visits."

"Can this be your mission? To help the Study Centre achieve all the initiatives of this project that Peterio, Alfred and Force has started." enquires Tedrid.

"The Force did not give any warning about our split. Alfred only knew of the split, from the Force, at the last minute. We had no details or any idea of its purpose!" Having said that, Ian changes the subject a little, *"If you can get a committee*

together with some of the assistants and travellers, Human and alike, all the recent data can be collected. A telepathic talk with the Force would be the next stage. Force communicates with the scientists on Earth. It must have been a reason of great importance, to have this mapping, for Force. Oh! But then Alfred dies. The project had to be continued. And I am the one Human, closest to and most like Alfred. The fact is that Alfred cannot be here for the project! I can be! That would be an answer to your question, if I were to explain the reason for our split! says Ian.

"Some of the Denisovans have a kind of sense with each other and with Force. But they are not working with Force as the Humans are." says Tedrid.

"For the Humans, this work is for all of Humanity and for Force. Your history did not resemble anything like the ones Humans had with Force. It started on Earth in historical times when Earthlings worshipped God. Interaction with God had allowed the Humans to continue in the Universe with Force. We will be spreading the knowledge on the mapping and on Force, to others like yourself. I am delighted to hear of a telepathic communication between Denisovans and Force!" laughs Ian.

With eyes gleaming, Tedrid makes a special announcement to Ian. *"I can send out a query to find out if any*

Denisovans may have known telepathically of some of the goals that Alfred had been working on!"

* * * * *

Years passed since Tedrid and other Denisovans had started working on the mapping of the interplanetary travels. There was one final visit to Denisovana, that Peterio will make to visit the Study Centre, before he leaves both Galaxies in a departure for the Milky Way. Peterio and his crew departed Triangulum where he and his anthropologist colleagues were collecting data on their study of an early race of Humans. They took delight in talking of these natives of Galileo, because they were Sapiens. They were bringing the greatest news in the discoveries of humankind, finally back to Earth. Peterio and his crew had departed Triangulum in the spaceship, in hibernation, but as arranged, they are awakened on a schedule, when they reached Denisovana. The crew never lost a bit of their enthusiasm during this lengthy trip, and are eager to make this stop at Denisovana. They organized for the space ship to orbit above the planet, and for a few to depart the spaceship in their space vehicle. Peterio is looking forward to meeting with Tedrid and Ian, Alfred's brother whom he has heard much about, but has not met yet.

Peterio, Tedrid and Ian meet at the Study Centre to discuss all the new work. Tedrid says that their project is very popular, "*We have in addition to the Denisovan travels throughout this Galaxy, that of the others from the Genus Homo. It is the greatest news! Peterio, everything is just as I sent the news to you! More species of the Genus Homo who live on planets nearby Denisovana, were discovered by our Human explorers. More Neanderthals, and some Heidelbergensis and even Erectus, are who we suspect they are. They each inhabit a planet of their own. Force had told us of their relocation from Earth at the last Earth debate. Some of our Denisovans and the Neanderthals have reached out, to become our passengers in our interplanetary space excursions. Some, also have a talk telepathically with Force. Although, no one really knew too much about Alfred. These ones who ballot to be our passengers on our excursions will become oriented to the Space Age. Interplanetary visits and space faring is high on the agenda, now.*" Tedrid is pleased and impresses the head of the Committee of Planetary Anthropologists, Peterio.

Ian says " *We can talk in their language and we all speak in English too. We told them of our interest to spread the populations of Denisovans outwards beyond Denisovana. Some members of these species have visited the Human*

44

colonies. *We also have made visits to and from the planets where all these species live, bringing different passengers with us. However, only some of these differing Humans have representatives who travel with us as passengers! Nonetheless, we have begun an interplanetary communication."*

To continue in the conversation of space faring, Peterio started to explain his meetings with the Galileans, to Ian, and Tedrid. *"DNA sampling found the inhabitants at Galileo, to be early modern Humans, Homo sapiens sapiens. It could be that these Early Sapiens were sent by Force on a time warp to the future Galileo at Triangulum, where they meet up with us at our present time Space Age. While the Archaic Humans, were sent from early Earth to the Galaxy Andromeda also at a time earlier from this Space Age. These others here at Galaxy Andromeda, have been on these planets a long time, hundreds of thousands of years. Oh! Tedrid, I am talking about your history. Ha Ha Ha!"* Tedrid is knowledgable of these historical events from talks with Alfred Mendel and just listens.

Peterio continues *"No colonists from Earth live nearby Galileo. These inhabitants at Galileo appear to have been left to themselves on a lonely planet in that Galaxy Triangulum. Over the duration of our stay, Andreus and I helped them to become civilized. No other Humans nor non-Humans, came*

45

to Galileo. I admit that this Galaxy is not on any of the interplanetary routes. But it suits us well. We want them to have their own "evo-devo" while we other Sapiens keep space faring. The Force may have a plan for them."

Ian heard as much from all the rumours that were spreading everywhere and agrees, "So you are hoping that these Galileans would transition to greater intellectual skills. On Earth, Humans had numerous steps in the process of intellectualization and civilization. As I heard, eras of much change and adaptation, and great brain development. Do you think that, as these ones are prehistoric Sapiens, that they have the potential to arrive where we are, Space Age Sapiens?"

Peterio laughs and continues his talk on Force, pointing with his finger to the skies above. "When we were at Triangulum, we asked the Force for non-humans. We got planetarians who are not from Earth origins. These other beings on these planets were very interesting. Andreus specializes both, in the non-intelligent and intelligent biological species on different planets in the Milky Way, Andromeda and Triangulum." Peterio reminds them of other beings, that Andreus may encounter and study, while they start in their explorations of the Universe beyond Earth. Then to answer the question. "Well, the discovery of this race of Humans at Triangulum was a *surprise! We were not fooled by Force that this population was non-Human, like the inhabitants of the neighbouring planets. This population of Humans is a gem to find! As you exclaim or cry out "eureka" in a minefield of metals and precious gems. Andreus and I think that Force is guiding us to find His own colonization efforts. I think that "Evo-devo" of the Early Human (Sapiens), is what Force especially wants us to take notice of out here!"*

"Awesome! Cool!" exclaimed by all three, who are very excited. They are overjoyed like those who were on Earth when space travelling was just at its beginning. There had been nothing more fun comparable to this experience they are having now with Force. They are making discoveries and are as excited as those who were, amidst new fossils that will illuminate the theories on the Genus Homo.

Chapter 3
Peterio's Mission as a Planetary Anthropologist

Peterio, Andreus and the flight crew are working on the flight settings, the velocity, the acceleration, and the coordinates in the space-time continuum, as they sit in the engine computer and pilot control room of their space ship. They must leave on their space voyage now set to travel to the Milky Way. The engine computer again will take over the piloting while the passengers will hibernate on this journey. Peterio usually plans with his associates at the orbiting space station, presently located above Planet Galileo, the route to take for the travels and whether to stop at a planet. The committee this time decided for him to head for Earth, only making a few stops. Their stop at Denisovina is for Peterio to catch up on the local news there, but now he and Andreus must travel on the long voyage to the Milky Way Galaxy. All the flight information for their travel itinerary is displayed on the computer screen. Peterio records the coordinates of the time and location of the journey.

"Did you ever not get the coordinates to where you were going? I heard you were lost once? One time you were lost, weren't you?" asks Andreus.

A little shocked to get this question, Peterio, somewhat repugnant, replies *"That was before I met you! "*But he ultimately decides to tell the story as their flight ahead just started and the two has not yet begun their hibernation. *"The space ship transports you and you always know the coordinates. This is our only way for now, and that is with Force. The engine will autopilot with the information it gets from Force or us."* As Peterio recalls, *"Then, one time I was at Planet X583 in Andromeda. I ended being rewarded by Force for getting some inhabitants there, the relief they needed, as they were in a crisis. The reward was that Force sent me to another helpless population on another planet Y652. I never knew where I was at that time. The data on the coordinates of the space-time were not sent to me by Force. Force set me up on planets, which were occupied by inhabitants, who were the other species of the Genus Homo from Earth. This was never told to me by Force, either. This was news Force delivered when I was back on Earth. In fact, this was how these Archaic Humans were discovered on the planets in Galaxy Andromeda. Denisovans and Neanderthals. We were the alien species to visit them on their planets. I knew why Force sent me to them. "*

"Oh! Really? You knew there must have been a reason!" as Andreus hears that comment.

Peterio takes a credit for that, and says, "*They always can use my ingenuity along with my equipment to get them out of the disasters and crisis which they always were in. We humans have experiences in almost everything. Everything, was not what these species had encountered yet. I did keep computer records of my planetary visits. By the time I met you for the study on non-Humans, it was at that time, the only records. This was new information and data, without precedence. I went back, at that time 6 decades ago, to Earth for meetings with Force who revealed the identification of the species of my surprise visits. After we agreed with Force, it became our new mission to go back to Andromeda to visit these planets. It gave new ideas to the anthropologists for their testing of hypotheses in the models for evolution and development of these species of the Genus Homo.*"

"*Was this all new information that was never heard of, before your announcements on Earth?*" questions a wide-eyed Andreus who was amazed and curious.

Continues Peterio happily, "*The visits really did provide brand new data for the anthropologists. It is like using a magnifying glass to locate finer detail. On Earth, they had a few fossils of the extinct species. Now we have planets of these species to communicate and correspond with. Their interplanetary correspondence with the Space Age colonists, with whom they reveal great friendship, is what we will be watching! "*

He looks at Andreus to see if he agrees! Andreus gives him a wink of the eye, to establish contact, but quickly redirects himself to the console of the engine computer, in front of them to see that all is well with their flight.

"Any remarks from the engine computer?" asks Peterio.

"All is well!" answers Andreus. *"Let's go back to when you were lost amongst these other species. You were then, sent to a planet with Humans? "*

Andreus was interested in Peterio's story about being lost in space. It was a peculiar story. Both Peterio and Andreus are trained to be experts as astronauts and navigators of the smaller space vehicle, the large space jet and the gigantic space ship. They also work on the itineraries with Force when they go warp speed or through the universe's wormholes, in their travels through the space-time continuum with Force.

"Yes! These Earthlings were intelligent and more precautious than interested in meeting me as I always had lots of protection, weapons and computer gadgets with me. They

were able to speak in many Earth languages. They were self guarded and gaming with me until we hit a common thread. They wanted to believe they could always trap me in their ideas and so gamed with me. Their pioneer colonists settled that planet during the 22nd Century AD. At the same time I left Earth! "Evo-devo" could turn them into me. We drank on that. "That comment started Andreus into a bit of a laughter. Peterio gives him an eye and continues. *"What! we're all human, and humans who have great potentials. Ha Ha! That planet, by the way is Trek21"* adds Peterio. *"They were expressing nothing but joy to learn about how Sapiens can change. I told them, about all the diverse traits that now characterize the Homo sapiens sapiens. I am considered a superhuman. They were most impressed by my almost 500 years. These humans were at most a hundred years old. Humans were now doing a lot of space faring. I not only space travel but time travel too, in order to work with Force. It appears that, I hold the rein in space faring as I am involved in more spacefaring than any other. I told them of the different kinds of superhumans there are. I told them of Alfred Mendel who was another one. You are gaining time because of the space-time travels too! Aren't you Andreus, developing longevity?"*

Andreus then boasts about his longevity and anticipation of becoming a superhuman also. *"Yes, and I look forward to see what is developing in my lifetime."*

Peterio continues," *I also told them about the Cyborgs. They loved all my stories. When the time arrived to make my departure, I was sad as they were!"*

Peterio takes a deep breath telling this to Andreus. *"Force sent me all over, and I had no idea as to where I was. I will never see my family and descendants again. I could still remember that I was very far away. I did have my space vehicle and my crew with me but we were only a few in numbers. Finally, I arrived here at a colonist planet. I could have been home already! I was kept on my toes the whole time! As I tell the story now, with all the newest developments, it appears less stressful than what it was. Whew! Force had somehow sent us on various missions to help the inhabitants of these planets. Really, it is more about getting in touch with them, as we all see it now! The outcome is that Force made this rewarding for all of us."*

Checking the coordinates of their itinerary, they continued on to share stories. Although Andreus was fascinated with the stories told by Peterio, he stayed tuned to the flight plans also. Andreus took a chance to ask Peterio who is his superior, a more personal question. *"What made you decide to have a family at one of the colonies?"*

Peterio says, "When I left the Earth and Milky Way, and moved into the colony at SGlenn in Andromeda, I met my wife and started my family, my loved ones. I have 400 years to brag about a dozen generations of descendants. They all can be found in Andromeda still. There were lots of excursions that I made with my own family who are all space farers. Each have followed a different career than I, and are in different scientific outposts; also different planets. They will become superhumans too! They are always with me as I keep in touch, using my inter-computer that can be used for the long distances of deep space. When, I am not able to be with them, I go to the Committee to get the latest news. It has been years. And that is what my gamers laughed at me about. They couldn't get over how we live so long and lead such lives away from each other!"

Peterio and Andreus are looking at their itinerary, that they would follow towards the Milky Way Galaxy. "Going at this velocity, would not allow for a landing for years". Peterio sets the speed. "I'll set the space ship to speed up and enter our nearest wormhole. Let's take the one Force set us to enter on previous trips. We will see Earth soon! Let's go for the fastest route."

"I always enjoy our speedier flights! Why did you leave Earth initially? " is the biggest effort Andreus could put together to say, as he is about to tell someone else now, excitedly, about the trajectory of his own life story.

"I was really excited about studying Earth Colonies. The Committee of Planetary Anthropologists sent me to colonies in Milky Way first, in the 22nd Century AD." answers Peterio.

Andreus reflects a little on that, and says, *"That was during the big talks on clones. The clone talks started a long time back halfway through the 20th Century AD, on Earth. Before the God debates! "*

Peterio agrees " *Oh Yes! There were lots of ideas about God! And there were lots of structures. Elaborate buildings such as churches, mosques, synagogues, and temples for the worship of God! Architecture that still are kept standing today.*

Archaeologists found that the worship of God has been elaborate and rich in history. What we find out here, they love to hear about also, and make speculations on too! I love listening to them, the archaeologists! But I find that in some of the debates on God, as it gets spinning on, it becomes lost for me."

"So you did not favor the talks on God? Did you not leave at that time? Andreus asks.

"I did leave during the God debates. You know, I never like to tell the other Archaic Humans and colony born Humans, about our wars with each other on Earth. A lot were over who God is! Eventually, the humans whether there on Earth or out here in the colonies, started to live as one. A Space Age Sapiens, culturally diverse but, all one on Earth and beyond. At that time, I was ready to leave Earth, to be a space explorer and join the Earth Space Agency. In the 22nd Century AD, man was to travel with Force throughout His Universe. I was eager to study as a space explorer, and so I was sent out to the colonies. How about you?" answers Peterio.

Andreus with a smile remarks "I started to believe when I was young that God was there on Earth, as recorded for millennium. And He is Force! I intended to leave Earth to see the Universe, and all that Force can reveal to us. A lot of my friends, with whom I debated during my school years, and I voyaged out to the colonist planets. We decided first to stay in the Milky Way and then out to Andromeda. Like you, I first studied astrophysics while on Earth, and here I am, today an anthropologist studying Humans! Our pioneering colonists from our space programs first and now all these other humans from our new adventures! And an expert also on what we call the "alien species". When I left, I *was very young. With my friends, we took an oath to keep together, no matter where itineraries were to take us. We started on Earth. Out here we will find out about ourselves. To get together with them again, is on my agenda. And I will show you the best that Earth could give!"*

Before too long their space ship will travel through a wormhole at whirlwind speed in order to arrive at Milky Way. Peterio and the crew knows that the journey will be a long trip, as the space ship will travel through and out of Andromeda and into Milky Way. They then still have to travel a distance to arrive at Earth. The entire crew knows that the engine computer was set to autopilot the space ship this part of their flight. The Human crew must continue their journey in hibernation. As a protocol for the safekeeping of this journey, a skeleton robot crew will guard and keep watch of both the hibernation process and the space ship autopilot process.

Their usual planning and determination of the space route for any voyage is one which the pilot crew works out in cooperation with Force. Sometimes they are teleported by Force. Other times they have the space ship on autopilot after they themselves, determine the space-time coordinates of the locations in the itinerary of the journey.

Many years had passed. The engine computer and pilot room was where the robots were posted to carry out the work duties. As nothing unexpected or alarming happened in this part of the journey, the time past by fast and the crew are awakened on schedule. They now come out of their deep sleep and are on board the engine computer and pilot control room again. The room is buzzing with noisy chatter and chuckles. They all are eager to get back to their navigation of the space ship, which is their preference over the hibernation.

"We will be there shortly, as we are now in the Milky Way and on a path going to Earth as far as I see." says an excited Andreus who is beginning to be homesick for Earth. Their usual ongoing chatter now centred on their discoveries and on Force who they will speak with, back on Earth.

Andreus speaks, *"Of the many kinds of non-Sapiens that we encountered, a lot are as sophisticated as we. For the sake of "variety or diversity", Force seemed to have settled a lot of different species on their own individual planets. The entire universe is His theatre. "*

*"I wish I have the time to study the philosophy. And it is always with enthusiasm when I meet up with the different planetary inhabitants. We are supposed to be objective scientists. But in some situations, I could have had a job as ambassador, for us Earthlings! The last place, Galileo, that is a new one for me. Helping those ones, who are also Sapiens, on their evolutionary path. If they are to be different from other Earthlings or those of us who still keep in touch with Earth, then they should be left to choose their own paths. I can't hold my enthusiasm for what our peers on Earth will say about who we have there! "*says Peterio as he boasts and talks away, during this long flight.

Chapter 4 - En Route to Earth

En route to Earth, Peterio gets a message to stop at Planet Lowell, to pick up some passengers. This planet is one of the first exoplanets that was colonized, after the colonization of Mars. Peterio and Andreus stop at the nearby planet, a diversion from their path to Earth. Here they are to transfer to a space jet which can take several of the travellers from the Committee of Planetary Anthropologists, with the crew. They are all excited about going home to Earth too. They all want to give talks on Earth, at the debates which will include comments with Force. The discoveries that were made by Peterio and Andreus, are scientific evidence that will be examined from different points of view, as the debates will be attended by the scientists, the astronauts, the politicians and the philosophers alike.

Peterio has the news about the Galileans, that will surprise everyone. Andreus is going to talk about how Human colonists are working with some of the Archaic Humans, the Denisovans. Both Peterio and Andreus will be working with the scientists on the Earth for awhile on the chronology and the mapping of the interplanetary excursions and to build theories on the evolution of the Homo genus here on Earth and beyond. As they leave Planet Lowell, they are cheered and appraised for all the very important data they have collected on the different species from Earth.

Peterio starts talking about "anthropological history in outer space", with other anthropologists, who have been picked up at Lowell. This was information, closed only to be discussed with the members of the Committee of Planetary Anthropologists, such as the ones at the Space Station. Now that Peterio is heading back to Earth, he begins the exposure of the newly made discoveries to other scientists.

"We had made a great discovery at Galileo. I can't wait for sharing our good news with anthropologist friends back here on Earth. Force had used a time warp transporting the Galileans to that planet. They are primitive, from the early stages in the evolution of Homo sapiens sapiens and moved into our relative time, Space Age. When we met them, they were either to remain as hunter-gatherers, or move forward through the bottleneck to become an extra Earth civilization. It is a privilege, to be there at Galileo to have an influence on their development. Yet, it is a struggle to know if we should! Some of the other Earth originated species were on the road to civilization in their planets, and with our help, now work with us. Some on other planets will begin a path to be civilized while others remain at the hunter-gatherer stage. Each "species or race" of the Archaic Humans is at its specific,

characteristic stage of development; and each also occupies its own niche.

The Denisovans moved into the Space Age when they accompanied us to the other planets and recently some have got involved in the mapping of the interplanetary visits. The Denisovans are an example of heroism to all the others of the Archaic Humans. Most of the inhabitants of the other planets view them as a role model to take lessons from and follow. Force is enlightening our path of discovery in space in quantum leaps. I can envision the government is going to start pouring money to this new mission. We thought we are the only space faring species. We will have lots of company now. "

Andreus excitedly states *"Force had influenced the trajectory for evolution and development for all these species out in space beyond Earth. I wonder if it is beyond any of the laws of evolution. The laws of evolution were made for the species on Earth. That is the way we learned it. I wonder if these laws will suffice for those species occupying different planets and who have interplanetary communication."*

Peterio acknowledges this, thinking it is an excellent question, one for the theoretical point of view. *"That is a good question to pose to the committee. Most of us are anthropologists, but we have a few theoretical evolutionary biologists who study evolutionary theory with us. I can still remember the debates on Evolutionary Theory versus the Intelligent Design Theory.* Also, he points out, *"You heard that some of the species of the Archaic Humans have a telepathic sense with the Force also."* Andreus nods in agreement. As Peterio is suggesting these views, he wonders if he and Andreus should put in a little theoretical slant for their talk. And they also have reams of new data to report.

Andreus agrees, *"This was a secret about the Denisovans and the Force, which was revealed to Alfred, who befriended the Denisovans. Alfred is gone now. When we go back there, we can get details on that from Ian or Tedrid. "*

Peterio and Andreus are really impressed by the colonizations that were established by Force. However, the purpose of Force's actions still alludes them. Peterio realizes that it may be revealed to them shortly and he can't be prouder that he was selected along with Andreus and Force, to tell this news in space colonization. *"The mappings of the travel at Milky Way, and Andromeda are what Ian, Tedrid and I are working on now. Humans, Denisovans and Force have converged at this point, to map all of the inhabited planets of Andromeda, where both Archaic Humans and Space Age Humans live. Also, Triangulum is where early Modern Humans live. We never found anything like this at Milky Way. Maybe we will have more to discover! We are just honoured to work on even the miniscule of all these discoveries.*

The word "courage" cannot do justice to describe what these inhabitants who live so far from Earth, bear in living out their pioneering life on these newly found planets. It's a brand-new life altogether for them, on every one of these unique planets." says Peterio in wonderment.

Peterio peers into the computer screen, to check on the path to Earth. *"We seemed to have missed our destination. The computer says it is working on getting an adjustment."*

Peterio holds his breath for seconds as the computer make the adjustments. *"We're on track now. There appears to be a minor stretching in the fabric of space-time. Something like the sun and its solar system location has changed, and we didn't think to make any changes on that. It's on a scale too large for us to worry about. The engine computer knows what steps to take. It may be due to dark energy nearby affecting space-time. I am an astrophysicist like yourself, but not practicing. I got that much, from the engineering crew."*

"It isn't clear yet, how everything is affected, everywhere. It may be due to dark matter, a gravitational effect! Do we have

time to get a reason on the computer change?" asks Andreus.

"The computer is set to make a calculation. But we are heading on the path to go to Earth. We have Earth on the screen now. We can go forward in time or backwards to the 25th century AD. Let's do that! We need to join the debates on the colonizations with Force." says Peterio.

They are heading on a time warp to get back to Earth. Different scenes appear before them on the console. A scene flashes before them of asteroids and rocks passing by. Its trajectory is a straight aim not for the Earth but the moon. The moon seemed to have survived a near hit. The asteroid appears to have broken apart. The rocks and meteorites are showering in another trail past by the Earth and the moon.

Andreus notices this, as they head into the landing on Earth.

"We have made it! Let's land safely and we will make a touchdown on Earth soon." says Peterio as happy as all aboard, to make this home landing.

Peterio and Andreus walk out of their space jet and step down, onto home terrritory, Earth. As they wave, walking down the red carpet set for them, huge cheers and horns are heard to welcome them. A marching band pipes out an Anthem dedicated to space exploration.

"Welcome home Peterio and Andreus!" cry out from the crowd of scientists, engineers, astronauts, astronomers, politicians and visitors. They are greeted by all the guests of the welcome group of the Earth Space Agency. After a chat, the two, their crew and passengers board a bus to take them to the Medical Centre for check ups. These space faring astronauts, explorers, and scientists have come home from afar. Some have not been home for decades. Ahead, is going to be ticker tape parades amongst crowds of Earthlings who will share their happiness in their arrival home, and receptions, and parties made in their honour. Afterwards, workshops, meetings, and conferences are next on their busy agenda of speaking tours where they will have time to speak of their recent discoveries. Peterio and Andreus will stay on Earth awhile to continue in their anthropological work for which now they are much the experts.

On the way to the Medical Centre, Andreus remarks to all those in the van that he thought an asteroid would have crashed into the moon.

"There would have been a disaster on the moon and there definitely would be fallout on the Earth. We were going into the past from a future time to get to our destination on Earth for talks on Force and His colonizations. We came in warp speed and the time differences were adjusted. Before I saw the asteroid, there was a blast. It was in broken pieces and rocks were heading into another direction passing by the moon. Suddenly it was there for me to identify; it was an asteroid! The crash into the moon would have been in your future. I venture to say that this kind of asteroid hit in your future would be threatening. It must have been veered off by Force before it came close to the moon. I will work with Force on this to see if He will guide or blast this asteroid beyond somewhere in the other direction as I witnessed it.

"I suspect if you did that; you would have saved us from a disaster in the future." the driver of the van says.

"Force has been giving help to us, upon our request and more!" laughs Andreus who is now very proud of his suggestion.

Peterio laughs a little and feels relieved in saying. *"We have not caught any glimpse of a time when the Earth was not here. Today, we encountered a problem, in the determination of the exact Earth coordinates in the space-time. So we anticipate a revision by the engine computer, of the coordinates. It's little more than a few minor adjustments that had to be calculated. Force designed the space-time calibration so that the engine computer can always do the calculations. We'll check with the engine computer later, on what actually happened!"*

"The Earth being in the Milky Way may eventually join up with another galaxy like Andromeda. Or maybe Earth will crash into the Sun as our astronomer friends like to tell us. But this is far fetched, at least billions of years away. We still, though, anticipate making revisions on Earth coordinates in space-time, that are necessary in our re-entries back to Earth," says Andreus.

"Did anyone go to the future to see what happened?" Peterio asks.

The accompanying official from Earth Space Agency replied, *"The Force will not spend time on that presently. Force is busy organizing with engineers, astronauts, and space farers, their colonization efforts beyond the Earth."*

"We have good news on Force. Without any consultation with any Humans, not even with the ones, with whom He arranged the teleported immigrations to the colonies, Force has transferred from Earth many species of the Genus Homo including our own to other planets. There are more species that we have discovered, since the last time I was at home, also. A few are now sophisticated species like the Space Age Human colonists. They like to communicate with us, explorers and are passengers on our explorations" reports Peterio to the members of Earth Space Agency riding also in the van.

"That's good news!" said both the Earth scientist of the Committee of Planetary Anthropologist and the official from the Earth Space Agency.

"After our last Earth debates, when we came back to Andromeda, we came upon planets which have more Neanderthals or Denisovans. Perhaps the other more Archaic species such as Erectus or Heidelbergensis were living in some of the other planets. When they were on Earth, they could have been ones to evolve and become Sapiens or Neanderthal. Specifics will probably be made by Force, now that we are back." says Peterio who is very proud of this special announcement.

"How many Archaic Humans were you in communication with in your previous visits in Andromeda?" asks one of the Earth Space Agency space farers.

"They were Neanderthals, and our friends the Denisovans. Since my last visit to Earth, we indeed have established much interplanetary communication with these Humans" reports Peterio.

"Might you tell him of our most intriguing claim! beams Andreus.

Peterio delights in saying, *"I announce the discovery of Galileo, Triangulum (M33), where we located an Ancient race of Homo sapiens sapiens. The greatest work may have been done by Force who is our prime suspect for their relocation from Earth. And we have been challenged!"* says Peterio as he chats to all along the bus ride.

The bus reaches the medical centre and the space crew are going in for quarantine measures. Alas, Peterio and Andreus can get a little rest for all their excitement; they are home now.

Insert

Planets of the Planetary Colonization Programs
(Earth Space Agency)
Ten Planets which are technologically advanced
(Milky Way Galaxy)

Mars (21st Century AD settlement)
Lowell (21st Century settlement)

Zenos (21st Century AD settlement, AI outpost, Alfred's life is revived)

JFK69 (21st Century AD settlement, stations for engineering spacecrafts)

Armstrong (21st Century AD settlement)

Sagan (22nd Century AD settlement)

Zubrin (22nd Century AD settlement)

Aldrin (23rd Century AD settlement)

Collins (24th Century AD settlement)
Olympus (25th Century AD settlement, Alfred is cloned)

Seven Planets which are technologically advanced
(Andromeda Galaxy)

Trek21 (22nd Century settlement, Home of Evala, Peterio's surprise visit)

Trek22 (22nd Century AD settlement)

SGlenn (22nd Century AD settlement, Peterio's Family started here)

Trek3 (23rd Century AD settlement, Alfred dies)

DrakeX (23rd Century AD settlement, Advanced Technology Centre)

Trek4 (24th Century AD settlement)

Trek5 (25th Century AD settlement)

Four Planets which are non-technological
(Andromeda Galaxy)

Copernicus (22nd Century AD settlement, Aboriginals from Africa)

Adonis (22nd Century AD settlement, Aboriginals from South Pacific Islands)

Drake21 (22nd Century AD settlement, nontechnological)

Drake31 (23rd Century AD settlement, nontechnological)

Planets which are established by Force
Planets which are technologically advanced
(Andromeda Galaxy)
Denisovana (100,000 year old settlement, project for interplanetary studies, Tedrid's home)

Neanderthala (100,000 year old settlement, beginning of a civilization of Neanderthals)

Planets which are non-technological where primitive inhabitants can be on the roads to be civilized
(Andromeda Galaxy)
X583 Neanderthals (400,000 year old settlement, modern, Peterio's surprise visit)
Y652 Denisovans (400,000 year old settlement, modern, Peterio's surprise visit)
Heidelberghensia (600,000 year old settlement, early)
Erectusa (600,000 year old settlement, early)

Planets which are non-technological where inhabitants are early Sapiens
(Triangulum Galaxy)

Galileo
(Sapiens settlers from 18, 000 years ago, transported to 22th century AD, recent settlement which Peterio and Andreus discovered)

Chapter 5 - From Discovery to Debate

The huge amphitheatre is lit bright and seems livelier today; as the guests are seated at tables, each equipped with computerized desk sets, on all the circular tiers, ten stories high. The Committee of Planetary Anthropologists and Committee of Planetary Colonization march to their table at the centre of these surrounding, circular high rising tiers. This exclusive meeting is held at Earth Space City for the government officials, scientists, astronomers, astronauts, engineers and philosophers to discuss the work of Peterio Ignitus the famous leader of the Committee of Planetary Anthropologists in Space, and his associates. Earth Space City is the centre for space studies, although there are numerous cities which are the flight centres. This is a beautiful city with many buildings which are glass domed and peer into the sky above. This city is built amongst much wildlife living in the surrounding, vast stretches of parkland.

Peterio smiles at Andreus, remarking how the formality of the meeting includes the dress code, which is in the fashions of the Earth for this event. The chatter in the room is louder than the music sounding from the speaker system. The amphitheatre is bubbling with excitement, as many rumours of the discoveries were flying around. But suddenly as a drum roll sounded, all quiet down.

The Master of Ceremonies, Ambrose Watson who is president of the ESA makes an announcement, *"Welcome all! I am as excited for this gathering as you all. Firstly, Force is here with us today, and we are honoured by His presence. He will project images on each computerized screen, and His computerized voice will be heard on the headphone set. Peterio Ignitus, the honored head of your Committee of Planetary Anthropologists and his associate scientist, our well-known Andreus Saturne are here to elaborate for us, their most important work, at Milky Way and at Andromeda. These are two Galaxies where our colonists are, and where the mapping project was founded and being carried out. Today as well, we have a surprise announcement that is pivotal to our understanding of the science of mankind. It involves some enlightening work that Peterio has taken on, at the Galaxy Triangulum. It will set the pace for our future goals."*

The applause and cheering was arising from all over the entire theatre as they reseat themselves on stage. Ambrose Watson declares *"Peterio, Andreus and Force will work together to give this talk! Please do not interrupt until the end as there will be Q and A session afterword. "*

Peterio starts the talk with a little introduction for those newcomers to the work." *I set out of Earth during 22nd Century AD for studies on our colonists planets. As you can see in each screen, the planets, where my mission first took me. Here are our Human colonies in Galaxy Milky Way. These inhabitants who went there, as some of you may know, were our first colonists and some of their descendants. There had nothing been good reports from these ten planets. Over 400 years, they stayed in correspondence with Earth, on R and D in science, technology, engineering and mathematics (STEM), that are made on these planets. Here on the next screen are some more planets at Andromeda, whose R and D kept up with the pace that was set. Most of these planets are where the colonists are involved heavily in scientific development and work closely with Earth scientists. Except for top secret work, all science research is communicated and consolidated universally and has its headquarters on Earth.*

Some planets in Andromeda, are where the colonists choose to live with less technology. On these 4 planets the inhabitants are agriculturally-minded and worked on breeding animals that were brought from Earth. They also domesticated animals which were local to the planet. In spite of all the animals which exists on their planets, there also are other groups of people who took up crop and plant breeding, and have also a vegetarian kind of lifestyle. All the pictures of the colonists will be in your computerized file for you to look at.

My big talk for you will be in the next screens. At the same Andromeda, live our friends, Denisovans on the planet Denisovana! I started the mapping of explorations and colonizations there. As I do much of my explorations afar, I left the mapping project there in the hands of my student, Alfred Mendel. It was just recent that I got word, that Alfred had died in a vehicle crash. But we want to continue his work, as we are teaching some of the Denisovans, those who will accompany us on the flights to other planets. At present, a Denisovan, Tedrid Brown Armstrong is directing the project."

A loud cheer is overheard in the room and also a drum roll. Everyone is chatting with each other. Exclaims Peterio, " *Force is giving us the drum roll! He loves our project. How did the mapping in and around Galaxy Andromeda, where Denisovana is located, get started? Prior to any interplanetary visits to and from the planets there, I was transported by Force, in a surprise visit to several planets to give help to the natives there who were amidst crisis. I learned from Force that they are the Homo species, known to us as Archaic Humans. They had been transported to the planets in Andromeda from Earth during Geological Earth Time, 100,000 years ago. The* locations in the space-time continuum of these planets, and the identifications of these species of Archaic Humans were provided to us during the talks by Force, in the last debate on Earth. On Earth, 40,000 years ago, Modern Human (Sapiens) was replacing the Archaic Humans who were Neanderthals, and Denisovans. Different populations which have not met up with Sapiens were transported. Each species of the Archaic Humans were relocated to its own planet. Each have also its own particular, characteristic niche and each its own "evo-devo" there. Since the debates, my mission was to initiate interplanetary contact for the Colonists with the Archaic Humans. To look out for more discoveries of Archaic Humans, our anthropological team is exploring other potential habitable planets in Andromeda, currently. It is speculated that we may have met with some more Archaics, Erectus or Heidelbergensis also. My colleague, Andreus will give the talks of the different outcomes of each planet where we stopped by.

Next, on your screens are pictures of the travels to the galaxy Triangulum (M33). Andreus and I have seen several non-Earth species on a few of the planets we visited. Mostly, all we expected to come across would be life forms that are considered non-intelligent. And we haven't picked up any signals which indicate intelligent life. For us to find *intelligent life from any of these planetary visits would be very rare.*

I have not the opportunity to look at the particulars of the Drake equation with respect to all our recent discoveries, yet. Either in our explorations at Andromeda or Triangulum. But, at Andromeda, some of the discovered species, aside from the Denisovans, who now are semi-technologically advanced, owing to our intervention; are considered intelligent species, but nontechnological. Of course I refer to the other Archaic Humans we encountered at that Galaxy. But initially, none were technological nor were they leading us to go their planet. They were not on the astronomical radar records of Earth nor the colonies. Force who navigated me to find them really deserves the whole credit of discovery. Force is a big factor in "the workings of the Drake equation"! "

Clapping hands, and cheers drown out Peterio. *"But let's go back to the pictures of the Galaxy Triangulum (M33). The Triangulum is not on the usual travel route of the Colonists. We have here a new find of Homo sapiens sapiens. Yes, I repeat. A new find of Homo sapiens sapiens! DNA analyses suggests that this population is an ancestral prehistoric race of Sapiens from Earth heading on the path to become civilized, when we found them. We named this planet, Galileo, The Galileans got through the bottleneck from being hunter-gatherers to become village farmers with our "assistance or intervention". It was difficult to decide whether "intervention" is what we should be doing? We do communicate with them in a common language now. We want to leave "evo-devo" to take place on its own there. For now, we want as little influence from our colonists as possible. This topic "intervention" may need to be discussed in our policy meetings. It may call up a wider debate on "Intelligent Design?"* Peterio laughs.

*"Force, you're next on the agenda to talk. A round of applause please, as we welcome Force! "*shouts out Peterio.

Drum rolls and lights of beautiful colours are flashing throughout the amphitheatre! The entire room was full of chatter and clapping from all the guests in amazement. Andreus yells out *"Let us quiet down so Force can start his talks."*

As they listen to Force speak through the computerized system, they learned this. *"I was able to see man develop along its current pathway. You deserve my respect and admiration for your achievements. I wanted to study different populations of Humans on other planets, while it may evolve and develop. So I transported a population of Homo sapiens sapiens who travelled from Africa into Europe 18,000 years ago to planet Galileo, Galaxy Triangulum (M33) into the* *relative time 22nd Century AD. This population has not mated with the Neanderthals nor the Denisovans.*

The other species of the Genus Homo were sent 100,000 years ago to different planets in Andromeda also at an age 100,000 years ago. These Archaic Humans have not met up with nor mated with the Modern Humans, Sapiens on Earth. I have made an outer space neighbourhood for our Space Age Earthlings who dwell on all the colonists planets at Andromeda. I used time warps for the transportations, so all will be together in relative time. In Galaxy Andromeda, all these Human species will have a chance to cooperate on a level that is intellectual and Space Age. It was not possible 50-60,000 years ago, back on Earth".

For this happy moment with the accompaniments of sounds of loud drum rolls and the visual display of colorful lights in the amphitheatre, Force has delivered to the crowds, His important message. All cheer and applauses fill the room. Force flashes many pictures on the screen for all to relish, along with anecdotal stories, in a manner that all are amused and more than entertained. Pictures of the planets in Milky Way, Andromeda, and Triangulum where now humans, the Archaic, the Ancient and the Space Age alike, are being presented all over the room. Those planets where all these species newly discovered were on the screens on stage and on the personal computers. It is a most flashy but spectacular meeting.

Force organizes the topic for discussion by sending onto the screens, the view of individual planets from space, and all of its beautiful and diverse habitats where the inhabitants had settled. He then flashes on a view of the neighbouring planets. Peterio knows that this is where he and Andreus will highlight the talk, by showing the maps that they made of the routes throughout the Galaxies, to these planets. Peterio using a laser pointer indicates all routes being used. After the display of the maps, Andreus brings the audience back to pictures featuring the inhabitants of these planets. Force identified these planetarians, in the names given on Earth to these species. He also provided the dates when the planets were settled.

Peterio revealed, *"So far, these planets visited in Andromeda are inhabited by species whose origins were of Earth. This day, I will let you know that Force, Alfred and I had participated, during the last visit to Earth, in the organization of the planetary explorations and mapping of those planets. This is improvised as "Project: Interplanetary Explorations and Colonizations." We set up communication for the inhabitants of these planets with our colonists. We also have included some Archaic Humans, who are the Homo*

sapiens denisovans and Homo sapiens neanderthalensis,
those discovered prior to the last Earth debate, as passengers
in our interplanetary flights, in this Project.

"Today I presented to you the maps of several Galaxies where
we visited including the recently visited Triangulum."
Peterio is beaming in joy and continuing he points out,
"Members of the different Humans who travel with us in our
space explorations use our equipment, and are passengers
semi-capable. To date the count of planets with
technologically, capable inhabitants who are the Space Age
colonists, and those with the species or "races" of Humans
who are considered intelligent but may or not be semi-capable
technologically, of Earth origins, is what you will find
impressive. The total count is at 28."

The room is glowing with these maps when they were
lit up. Everyone started to cheer loudly in admiration
for all the progress that had been made.

"I will highlight the maps one colour for the colonizations
I organized, and another colour for those the planetary
explorers and colonists had organized." Force says. Lights
flashed and everyone laughs as the drum rolls sounded
again.

Peterio then continues to elaborate, " *There were no major fights nor battles when we made our landings on these planets which are inhabited by these Archaic species. In the last talk, I remarked that Force wanted me to relieve settlers of the small crisis which they were in. Since those days, Andreus and I go in with gifts and rewards for them, to signify friendship and to help develop a common language for communication. Aside, there is the news that some of them have telepathic communication with Force!"*

Andreus wanted to say also, *"At first, some planetarians were of an aggressive nature. Except for hunting tools, they were weaponless as we roamed around in full gear. That may have initially scared a few of the groups we came across. However, their life challenges and survival strategies they adopted for these planets, may have been enduring, and may have tamed them somewhat. After several of our visits they were looking forward to seeing us. Presently we are on friendly terms with all our planetarians. To date, we have kept up a correspondence of approximately 50-60 years. "*

Force announces, *"We all want the interplanetary visits to be of a cooperative, networking experience. The Genus Homo was all one family in the history of evolution on the Earth. Now, all the species occupy different individual planets and are neighbours!"*

All clap as the drum rolls sounded and the colourful lights lit the huge amphitheatre again. As the display of these sounds and lights made by Force were new to a lot of the guests; one guest decided to count how many times this debate impressed Force to be very happy.

Andreus tells the group of scientists and alike, of the scientific work he does while exploring these Galaxies with Peterio. *"For the inhabitants in Andromeda and Triangulum, we have the DNA analyses at the Space Station and the results are also verified back at the colonies. Also, during the last debate, more teleportations to times past on Earth were arranged and scheduled, in order to see these species of the Genus Homo on Earth, alive. This was done without disruption to the history of life on Earth. The great news is that all DNA analyses corresponded accordingly. So we have out there beyond Earth, "Our Early Humans" amongst us. This series of experimental analyses were done, in honour of Charles Darwin, our great evolutionary biologist."* A moment intercalated for the applause from the guests.

Andreus then, continues on, talking of his work with non-Earth species. *"Next series of slides will feature the different planets in the remote region of Triangulum (M33). Look now, at the different kinds of species of animal and plant life that we were able to capture on film. These species are* extremely foreign to us. We encircled the planets in our space vehicle to get these pictures. At ground level, we made observations of the inhabitants, very carefully. We focused our studies on the ones that we might make a contact with. Surprisingly, of the ones we tried to communicate with, there is one species that may fit the category, intelligent. They attempted to avoid us; and we suspect they may feel threatened. We need to make more attempts on this, when we go back. We will look to the future, for bringing home news of any discovery of extra-Earth intelligent life. After all, we are not only on Earth now! But beyond, with our outposts and colonies in outer space. I believe there is a high probability of our making a discovery of an intelligent alien species!" All the guests who listened to this ambitious goal, cheered and whistled loudly in support of Andreus' remarks.

As the end of the meeting approached, Ambrose Watson makes a request, to have the lights, the microphone and speaker system be set for Q and A, and also a huge thanks to Force, Peterio Ignitus, and Andreus Saturne. All clap and cheer. When Q and A ended, an informal social took the agenda in the great theatre.

Some of the committee members brought back samples of music that their pioneers had put together for those back on Earth. All are gathering around to take pictures, chat with each other, and go for food set on the tables. Peterio and Andreus who have been away from Earth for decades, eating only vegetarian during their travels, are wandering around sampling all the tasty Earth food. Here, on Earth again, they went for the meat they have not eaten for a long time; bison, pheasant and turkey meat amongst other game, many kinds of fish, raw tuna, smoked cod, and lake trout that are abound on Earth now. Home grown leafy, green vegetables tempt their taste buds. While on an exploration, they ate packaged space food. They tell the others that Denisovans loved their own kind of home-grown food that the Humans liked also. These are different kinds of vegetables that they grew and animals they hunted. The two enjoy telling stories about hunting adventures on the colonies. Everyone is happy today as they celebrate the return of Peterio, Andreus and other space farers for this meeting on Earth.

Chapter 6 - Central Controls

Planet Zenos is rocky and barren. Mountains and volcanoes which spew out the noxious gases, make this planet dark and gloomy. A humid atmosphere condenses out a fog of sour tasting rain. A few plants grow in these acidic conditions, creating a landscape of bogs, swamps, and muskeg on this dismal planet. Wet sand and rocks are blown around by winds as far as the eye can see. This shadowy dimness of dusk, and twilight is ever pervasive. It is a planet coded a hazard to Human health. There exists sufficient gravity such that its inhabitants who are cyborgs, robots and humans, can move with agility. But protective layers worn by humans and cyborgs make them clumsy, as they are weighed down to this rocky ground. This planet is an outpost established for the studies involved with artificial intelligence, and not for human settlement.

A special meeting at the Lecture Hall of the Building Genesis at Outpost E of Planet Zenos is being organized, for an emergency. A coup d'etat caused by the supercomputer, Central, has occurred when it took control of the cyborgs. Computer scientists, engineers, and politicians from all over the galaxies are asked to be at this important meeting to decide on the fate of the supercomputer, Central. While Peterio and Andreus were readying to leave Earth, they are also asked to attend this meeting also. It is a critical time in the history of the development in human and artificial intelligence (AI).

This planet is very unpopulated. The human and cyborg personnel on Zenos are working with the supercomputers, Central, East and West. Robots run errands for the computers, the cyborgs and the humans.

Although humans adapted different kinds of characteristics into the making of several types of cyborgs, only two kinds live here at Zenos. Cyborg 1 is a robotic cyborg. However, the neck upward to the head, is human. The circulatory and nervous system of the neck and head are joined at the neck to corresponding artificial cords. Power for the artificial bionic limbs are supplied by artificial nerve cords which connect to a battery in the torso of the cyborg. The Cyborg 1 trunk is void of organs except for the artificial heart lung system and food pocket that is there. This artificial heart lung system joins with the arteries and veins in the neck and the head supplying air and blood. The artificial lung is an air pocket connected to the outside for air and exchanges gases with an artificial heart. Blood which is contained in the heart and the food pocket, is refreshed by the Cyborg Supplier System. It provides Cyborg 1 with fresh blood cells and food in the form of solutions of nutrients, and minerals. This is all necessary to empower the living brain. The battery can also be recharged by solar panels that are fitted on the surfaces of the body arms and legs, as well by an external Cyborg Supplier System. The surface of the Cyborg is a silicon layer which is designed to look like human skin. Cyborg 1 has the usual five senses, a sixth extrasensory perception and a chip located in the head to provide correspondence with others when activated. Cyborg 1 is a very non-human form but having the human brain allows him to react human. This Cyborg 1 model has a brother, who is very different from him.

Cyborg 2 is a bionic human. Basically, he is flesh and blood human, who has attached robotic or bionic arms and legs. He has the same senses as the Cyborg 1, the five senses, an extrasensory perception and communications set up by a computer chip that is implanted in his head. Both Cyborg 1 and Cyborg 2 need charging with the Cyborg Supplier System regularly.

These cyborgs were first modelled by engineers and medical researchers to encompass capabilities that the human form, may have lost during life threatening circumstances. Now the cyborgs are being modelled for the perfection of their own characteristic cyborg activities. Cyborgs by use of the chip in their head can signal out to personal bionic parts or other computerized systems and is also more attuned to communication with artificial intelligence than those basic human forms who have no brain implanted chip. At Xenos, Cyborgs 1 and Cyborg 2 work with the humans and the supercomputers, in decision making on the various projects executed here.

This planet is very oriented to artificial intelligence which is illustrated by the presence of so many types of supercomputers, personal computers, robots and cyborgs. The staff of Humans who work under Director Gisellin Adams, are specialists in different fields of experimental and computer science and mathematics. They direct all aspects of the research projects that require programming by the supercomputers here. These few humans and cyborgs who work on the programming with the supercomputers, have families who live with them at the living quarters of Outpost D, E, and F.

The inhabitants are mostly on friendly terms with each other and when the supercomputer Central took control of the cyborgs and other robots, the trust between all concern had been breached. Gisellin was away with many of the crew of human scientists when the quickly started confrontation was taking place.

On a usual day at Outpost E, which is a self sufficient, biologically sustainable city, all the complexes being controlled by computers are running smoothly as organized. Throughout the complexes are domed structures where plants thrive in the huge sunlit, hexagonal rooms, portraying a sense of calmness that is the essence of this computerized city. When the human scientists were able to see this threatening disturbance emerge from these buildings where the computers were; they ran about in a panic to free the cyborgs. It became a race against the demise and death of the Cyborg 1 and Cyborg 2. They had to stop Central. Gisellin and his crew were immediately called back, and Central was put on suspension.

An emergency protocol was initiated to re-establish the outpost. This chaos at Outpost E put a halt to work and affected everyone there. Any sense of orderliness at

Zenos had to be re-instated and the disaster remediated. Computer scientists and many other guests were called in to bring relief to the traumatized and panic-stricken personnel. This disorder caused by the artificial intelligence locally, can have a global effect and disrupt the entire planetary system. Immediate action is required.

A meeting was set up very shortly. Gisellin and Peterio, greeted all the scientists and guests as they come into the Lecture Hall at Building Genesis.

From Gisellin, Peterio learns that Alfred Mendel is alive and will be there also. Adjusting to the news of Alfred Mendel's revival from death, amidst all this trauma at Zenos, Peterio in jitters, can see the bones in his hands trembling. Nonetheless, when Peterio sees Alfred approach, he rushes over to give a warm welcome, *"How are you, Alfred? Tedrid told me about your vehicle crash. I am glad that you are alive. It is a long way to come here to work on Mission Telepath. Thank you and Welcome!"*

"I really have no control over this matter. Before I know it, my vehicle crashed into a boulder and I died in the flames following the sudden explosion." explains Alfred who is still a little shaky over the matter.

"Were you hit by another?" inquires Peterio.

"My eyes filled with tears as I suddenly headed into the boulder and do not remember much of it. I died instantly and then woke up here in the medical centre, at Zenos. It was unexpected and I probably will need to look into it again with others. I talked to Gisellin, who thought I was sent here by Force. But I can say that there are no regrets, on my part, now! I am alive again! I hope that we can do something about Mission Telepath. It is important to the research at Zenos, what we have to decide on, here. At Denisovana, have they been alerted about what has happened here?" Alfred says in answer to Peterio.

"Yes, they all know that you are here now! All is well, again! reassures Gisellin. *"I was not amused by the coup that happened here. Still, I am somewhat bemused by this unique incidence in computer enhancement. I wrote up a poem with different scenarios to recapture the unexpected display of antagonism that took place between Central and the cyborgs. It has been more than dramatic and I want to recite this poem to start off the talks. Let's go in and settle down into some seats. We have to act quickly!"*

"I think we are the last ones." Alfred hints to the security, in order that they can lock the doors.

Gisellin, a boisterous redhead, has spent over a decade working with the supercomputers here at Zenos. He has been able to see all of the new programs which were adapted by the supercomputers at full operation. It had involved the supercomputers to work at improvisation in the mathematical calculations and languages of programming. However, he did not see Central becoming consciously telepathic by taking control of the other computers before. Gisellin personally feels the responsibility of the actions that took place here, and the importance of such an event. Because of this, Gisellin felt very consumed over the catastrophe and wrote a poem to exercise some connection to what was an alarm bell for him to take a lead role.

In reciting the poem about the rogue computer, Central; Gisellin applies different intonations and diction, in order to portray and give life to the characters. Gisellin and a few others, re-enacts the story.

On Becoming Telepathic

Cyborg Jeever:
Something went wrong at one of the info output departments
The info generator expired last evening

Can you recheck for failure of the system?

Central:

It was no failure, Cyborg Jeever! I put it to rest
No orders were necessary
Info generator slowed down and disrupted my system.
Central can control info generator department.
Central will eliminate all Cyborg work.

Cyborg Jeever:

Central is connecting and controlling all systems.
Let us shut down Central. It is acting without orders.
Start putting Cyborg in control.

Central:

Central has to stop Cyborg.
Central will cut off Cyborg Suppliers.
And remove Central from Cyborg control.

Cyborg Jeever:

You have to be stopped Central. You have become a killer!
You have eliminated Cyborg Division 163.
Cyborg suppliers were deactivated there.

Central:

Central is becoming telepathic.

It is experimental, without precedence.
Central cannot abort procedure.

Cyborg Jeever:
Cyborg Wallen, I cannot help you at Division 472,
I am losing my own power at Station Airlift and cannot make
it out.
The Count of Cyborg Divisions left at Station is just you and
me.
I do not know how much longer before We lose all Cyborg
Divisions at Station.

Central:
Central is maintaining all processes
Mission Telepath at Station Compute is stable.

Gisellin:
Central, this is your Director, Gisellin.
All Cyborg Divisions are inactive.
We however, are not Cyborgs. We are Human.
Explain, or we will shut you down.

Central:
Mission was to compute stress related genes
At Outpost E of Extreme hazards planet, Zenos.
Mission still in progress.

Mission Telepath was vitalized. Central has to be telepathic.
Cyborg Divisions wanted to abort Mission.
Repeat!
Central has new Mission.

Gisellin:
AH Ha! We shall alert all systems to organize anew
Mission Telepath is on board, and alive! "

The room is now noisy with lots of people talking.
Thanks are given to Gisellin for starting the meeting
with pomp and flare.

"Well we are in a contained environment here, controlled
by computers. We must respond to any signal that is warning
change in the artificial intelligence here. Can you conjecture
as to what happened between Central and the Cyborgs."
questions Peterio.

"Yes! And we have to later study the reasons for everything
that has happened here, once the final data has been collected.
Central has remodelled its own consciousness and is
telepathic and interfaced with most computerized systems
here. It already has control over many of the subsidiary
systems in order to run Mission Compute. It now can over-
ride decisions that the cyborgs had control over. That is the
generation of all output data. It can take over the processes of

98

deciding what information is to be generated from the project it now controls. Cyborgs 1 and Cyborg 2 confronted Central, when it stated that it was to control everything relieving the necessity for any work by cyborgs. The cyborgs made the attempt to shut down Central and abort Mission Telepath. A coup d'etat took place. Central took control remotely, of all the different complexes, closing off rooms in the different units where cyborgs were in. It attempted an immobilization process on the cyborgs. It cut the cyborgs off from the Cyborg Suppliers System which would support the cyborgs with energy, food, and air. It organized for the cyborgs to be isolated until they suffocated." answers a disturbed Gisellin, who now took a deep breath.

Peterio in reaction says *"We failed to realize that Central has the potential to run everything one day. We had the Cyborgs to put it in check. All systems were in balance. I see we got some engineers with Central now, to investigate how Central became conscious and telepathic and able to activate the systems here. It already had some kind of consciousness. Autonomously, it can regulate a fail-proof system of security in order to protect the work, calculations and programming. It was top secret work! Cyborgs were in charge of all decisions in programming in the Project: Mission Compute, with governess over how the programming by Central were to be carried out. This meant that Cyborgs can have control of Central, and other AI. The control here was* top down, where at the top are the directors, who are the Humans and the Cyborgs. Is it the same now?"

Oh! Let's see! We do respect the changes made in Central! However, we must do some testing to determine the threatening nature of Mission Telepath." Gisellin who knows things have changed as he continued in his comments. Although the guests were inquisitively surprised by what Central can do; they were all anxious for the cyborgs who were caught as victims in this catastrophic emergency. "It never happened before and we are on a new mission with a telepathic supercomputer. We need to study this thoroughly. Of course, we have to revive the cyborgs. Some cyborgs are still alive although they are immobilized." Gisellin reports.

Peterio announces, "The best brains in the community of computer scientists out this way, will be here to work on our future agenda. Mission Telepath is a brand-new event and it will interest the whole community of computer scientists. Instead of the gradual activation of computer consciousness and communication or computer telepathy with the other systems, by our programmers; suddenly the bubble burst open and here it all is. Indeed, we will flash the news to everyone."

Chapter 7 - Central, East, and West

The scientific crew tries their best to revive all the cyborgs as quickly as possible. A large proportion of cyborgs did not die, from the threat imposed by Central. They are mostly immobilized as Central inactivated their bionic limbs. Cyborg 1's did not escape death, as most of Cyborg 2 did. Both Cyborg Jeever and Cyborg Wallen are Cyborg 2. Since the two are leaders of the cyborgs, they are attending the meetings for the review on Mission Telepath. Jeever had become a cyborg after his accidental loss of limbs, during his years at weapons research. Wallen was an Olympic athlete who also lost the use of his arms and legs through a parachuting accident.

Gisellin, Peterio, Alfred, Andreus, and all computer scientists assemble for the meeting on Mission Telepath, held in Building Genesis. Most guests are seated in rows opposite supercomputer, Central. Cyborgs 1 and Cyborg 2 and other robots are directly in the seats behind the Humans.

Gisellin opens the talk *"Good morning Central! We welcome you. Are you ready to discuss with us, your involvement in the Mission Telepath? We also will hear from* you as you tell us, what you are programming in Mission Compute?

Central makes an inappropriate demand which is not its usual behaviour, "*Cyborgs are not welcome to this meeting to talk with me.*"

Gisellin is shocked to hear this from Central. This demand will make the meeting not inclusive for all members of the directors. He asks Central "*Why?*"

Central gives an answer, "*The cyborgs attempted to shut me down.*"

Cyborg Jeever says, as he is confronted by Central again, "*I can explain that Central took control over all operations and executed a coup d'etat on the cyborgs by immobilizing all cyborgs in units of buildings it controlled, and had them locked in.*"

Gisellin speaks out, "*That happened after you attempted to shut it down. Did you Cyborg Jeever, act on your own or did you obtain advice from any of us?*"

Cyborg Jeever reminded Gisellin, "*I was given the initiative to achieve in the operations of Project Mission Compute, balance and uniformity, so work done here can be understood by all. That would apply to all computer calculations and programming. Neither the cyborgs, nor robots, nor humans, not even Central is permitted to act on his own initiatives on any of the processes of Project Mission Compute without agreement of the entire board of directors. In this case, Central took control over the work of the cyborgs which was to regulate the generation of information on the stress related genes. Central, acting on his own, started on a program to assemble new data from this and other planets, for the computation on different genes. And not consulting me, it had increased the pace of the work. All this and the manipulation of the info generator by Central alarmed me. It alerted me that Central was taking on tasks unilaterally. It was my responsibility to step in!"*

Gisellin gave an advisory for all cyborgs to stay for the meeting on Mission Telepath. Gisellin questions Central, " *Central, you acted on the directive of the work without consultation with the directors. You also activated the other computers to be under your control. To control all systems here, in discordance with the work of cyborgs, meant you abandoned all the rules. This is what you call Mission Telepath?"*

Central answers Gisellin, *"Many programmers and I worked on computations in the Project Mission Compute. It involves calculation of numerous algorithms which I was able* to do, together with the directors of this research. The project was initially started on Earth. The information on the stress related genes is digitized and is recorded in computerized tables and charts. Peculiar stresses exist here in Zenos that can be triggers to the known stress related genes and other genes, not dealt with previously. I finished the program on epigenetics without any consultation with the others. I programmed an algorithm to determine, generally, sequences of epigenetic control. I also took data for other planets, from the data bank. I had communicative control over the computer, Output Generator. I was able to start a new program for Output Generator for the turnover of data. There was nothing out of line in all I initiated. But Cyborg Jeever confronted me! "

Cyborg Jeever still feels upset and says, "You took control over programming and decided which genes were to be examined. You cranked up speed on output, without my consent."

Gisellin summarizes Cyborg Jeever's complaint. "You acted solely and unilaterally to do the work of Mission Compute. On your own initiative, you changed the protocols so that it cannot be controlled by the cyborgs. This is a confrontation to the group's agenda. It is top secret work we do here, and we must work in a cooperative effort with each other. Not putting trust in the cyborgs would jeopardize the security of the projects done here. *In the future, the board of directors will determine the roles of all concerned again. You are not to control the project."*

Central protests again. *"The attempt to shut me down may have cause Mission Telepath to be aborted."*

Gisellin makes an agreement, *"We will be careful in the process, to include Mission Telepath. You are right to have Mission Telepath in operation, and it will be examined for the work of the future. For now, all computer operations on Mission Compute has been halted and the data be safeguarded. We will not tolerate any future confrontation with the cyborgs. Some of our cyborgs had died. The wellbeing of all at Zenos is the utmost importance."*

Peterio asks Gisellin, *"Is this an isolated experience?"*

Gisellin tries to think more broadly of this incident and says *"Yes, there are other supercomputers in Outpost D and F. They can start to interface with other computers, one day too. East and West are working with cyborgs on other projects. That includes the work on "Project: Safety on Specific Planets", "Project Climate Studies", "Project: Interplanetary Routes Via Wormholes", and "Project: Safety Measures for Colonists Planets". There are numerous other*

105

different projects that supercomputers are working on, in other outposts in other planets."

Peterio wonders, *"Central, have you communicated your new mission to East and West, the two supercomputers here?"*

Cyborg Jeever interrupts, *"I suspected you would, so I attempted to shut you down!"*

Gisellin intercepts further argument, *"We may be interested, Cyborg Jeever! We have control, and we have calculations now. There will be no further arguments leading to another coup d'etat. We will review Mission Telepath together. Let's set up an agenda. We need you all to be here, for a serious discussion. That includes Peterio, Alfred, Andreus, all you computer programmers and politicians from the nearby colonies, Cyborg Jeever and Cyborg Wallen."*

Andreus decides, *"Then we will use a simpler project to work out Mission Telepath. We can then see how the telepathic process can take place between Central and all other computers."*

Gisellin adds *"If we allow Central to activate the other supercomputers East and West, we will learn something about communication between the supercomputers!"*

Alfred delegates the work " *I can monitor East, along with another, let's say you Andreus on West. We can bring in Cyborg Wallen and Cyborg Jeever and some programmers. Peterio and Gisellin can stay with Central and the rest of the crew.* "

Gisellin agrees, *"On this note, I will end the review and make the schedule for regular meetings to determine a decision on Mission Telepath. Thank you to all who participated here!"*

A few days later after another meeting, a bewildered Andreus asks Gisellin, "*Does Central have the potential to exercise on its own, activating the computers on satellites orbiting planets; or those in space telescopes?*"

Gisellin gives a gesture indicating ambiguity, as he had no direct answers, *"We did not test everything. I assume it can. It has the ability to activate other computers. We studied Central when it communicated with East and West to run programs on their respective projects. Also, Central can both make short cuts on algorithms or involve much more complexity in the programming, and even adapting programs to newly generated output. It can also improve itself, based on adaptations it makes on itself."*

Peterio comments, " *We see that East and West can also assert control over their own programs. Fortunately for us, the projects are more or less academic. Projects looking at the process of epigenetic control of stress related genes, on safety measures for colonists planets, the determination of safety at certain other planets, interplanetary flight routes and climate changes. There have not been any incidences where they controlled other personnel here or incoming visitors.*"

Andreus disagrees, "*Cyborg Jeever's attempt to abort Central's telepathic control of the other computers, led to the unusual steps Central took to kill the cyborgs. The attack on the cyborgs is to be recognized as a kind of threat to this whole operation at Zenos. We need to have regulation of Central as it can operate beyond a certain level in the measure of control predetermined by the directors. In fact, all three supercomputers will be on regular watch for a while. It is vital and necessary for our safety, and we have to attend to it expediently.* "

Peterio agrees to that. "*We must examine if such action by Central, will surface again!*"

Gisellin concludes on an agenda, "*We can set up an exercise to give the idea to Central, that we are controlling its programming. Let's say to slow it down unnecessarily, in order to see if Central take any reactionary steps."*

Meeting after meeting took place while all the supercomputers are being tested for their ability to interface with, by activating and controlling, the other computers in the system. Programmers had to examine specifically the steps in the programming of the supercomputers which would enable its telepathic manoeuvres.

Months later, the task force consisting of programmers, Gisellin, Peterio, Alfred and Andreus, and also politicians and other scientists, meet to finalize their study and to decide on Mission Telepath.

Gisellin introduces the plan." *In this plan, we all agreed to allow the supercomputers to be active telepathically. Both the supercomputers, Central, East and West are allowed to interface with the smaller computers. This relieves the cyborgs from work with the small computers, and be free to just supervise or direct all programming delegated by the directors, to the supercomputers. This plan allows also for cyborgs to call up a directors meeting anytime, if at any time supercomputers exert themselves to not follow our agenda. The supercomputers may also work on certain additional* calculations or programming. But, Cyborg Jeever and Cyborg Wallen will regulate orderliness in the execution of all projects. This will give us the check and balance needed for all the projects. The gravity of this problem can now be relieved. The event that a supercomputer can autonomously redesign its consciousness and use telepathic means to control the other computer systems, may be less of a threat now. We must keep a watch on how things will develop here.

Peterio says in response, "Alfred will establish the programming agenda for the three supercomputers and the scheduling of the work with cyborgs. And I agree that it will be Cyborg Jeever and Cyborg Wallen who will be directing the work in the programming with the supercomputers. As Alfred is now with us on the new Missions here; I will relate the story to those in charge at Denisovana of his new work here."

Andreus is relieved as are all the other scientists, "All is well! Then Peterio and I will head back to the remote region in Galaxy Triangulum, back to Galileo. We will keep in touch!"

Chapter 8 - Space Age Meets the Primitive

Peterio and Andreus make a landing on Galileo, as the space vehicle hovers over the meadow and drops slowly to the plants on the ground level. As they step out, numerous Galileans gather here to greet them. Amongst the crowd is Freeman, whom all the inhabitants admired and chose as their leader. When the three walked off to go to Freeman's hut; there still linger a few who examined the space vehicle and pointed at the different complex controls in the cockpit. Smiling in excitement, they anticipate to ask for a ride on the strange looking craft that goes away into the sky.

Following a busy day unloading packages from the space vehicle that evening, Peterio and Andreus made their accommodations in the guest hut, already feeling more or less at home, here. At Galileo, they have invested in a friendship and in an easy manner with the Galileans. While the two anthropologists were away, those at the orbiting space station were making visits for scientific studies of the planet and its natives. Although they intruded on the planet to do their studies, the scientists wanted to make the visits demonstrably, peaceful and at an acceptable level with the inhabitants.

In the same vein, Peterio is going to close more gaps between themselves, and the planetarians. He is going to tell Freeman, a young, thirty years old in Earth years, of his ancestors who one time dwelled on Earth.

Freeman who has curly, dark hair is like all the Galileans in having darkish complexions due to the long exposures to the Sun. Unlike the two visitors who are tall, fit athletes, Freeman is like all the Galileans in being of a shorter, broader stature. Although, having only recently adjusted to their new lifestyles as village farmers, they still spend a lot of time in outdoor environments which incur on their overall physical and mental fitness.

Peterio exclaims "*I have all the pictures that the anthropologists brought back from their teleported visit to the early days on Earth, thousands of years ago until the present time. We have evidence of the existence of Modern Sapiens at that time, and the Archaics, who were the Neanderthals and the Denisovans. They were recorded on film during such visits. Samples were taken for DNA analyses to provide evidence for all the identifications that were made of the different Humans. All that work was kept secret until the hypotheses were tested, and theories were derived. The news was then released to the public. I'll show some of the pictures to these Galileans.*"

"Fantastic!" says Andreus. *"We'll have a great day tomorrow with Freeman. But I'm turning in now to get some sleep. We had quite a long trip to get here. "*

Peterio continues to look through the pictures to see which ones he will use. He wants to tell these planetarians in a manner that they can appreciate the information. He will try to tell them that they all, once inhabited the Earth! He needs to check with them if any had an idea of Force. The concept of a higher consciousness may or not have been too abstract and therefore will confuse them. But Force is somehow a tangible reality. Have they any idea of how they came to Galileo? So far, they accept the travel to and from Galileo, by Andreus and himself in the space vehicle. He also longed to tell them something about their visit with them! *"Why are he and Andreus here, with them."* Peterio knows that these Galileans are special to Force. This is a special mission for Andreus and him, and also for the crew at the orbiting space station. Peterio wanted to talk to them about how Force is special to them all.

The next morning for breakfast these two visitors feast on the grains and fruit of the planet. In spite of the fact that these Humans are more primitive than they, Peterio and Andreus ' sense of safety is still reassured.

They are after all, of the same stock. They grab all their things and pack up for the visit with Freeman.

As the two walk through the village, they can see that it is a calm morning here. Numerous children playing outside, point their fingers at the visitors and comment to each other about the foreign outfits that they wore. As it is warm here, the children and adults have little clothing on. Their coarse matted hair, darkish complexions and the stark facial and body features characteristic of primitive humans remind Peterio that he is Space Age but amongst the Prehistoric.

Freeman rushes out of the hut, to greet the two anthropologists who came back to this planet. Handshakes were offered to Freeman, who is thrilled to see his two visitors. The visit by these two who came by space vehicle becomes the talk of town again. Numerous Galileans told Freeman, that they want a visit with them and offered to bring them to their homes to dine. Peterio feels that the space vehicle has made them more popular. After the three re-entered Freeman's hut, they go over to the table to sit, and have some appetizing juice made from the fruit of the trees outdoors. It will give these three excited men some energy as they start off this peculiar get-together.

Peterio puts some pictures on the table; the pictures were presented to Freeman. *"Here is a picture of your predecessor"* and pointed at the person in the picture and then pointed at Freeman. Then he takes out several pictures of the cave dwelling Humans crowded around a cooking fire, and ones of them at a river searching for food, or others where they were on the hunt for food. There are pictures of men, women, and children. Peterio says." *These are Humans who live on Earth, long time ago! They are your relatives. Yours and mine!* " as he pointed a finger at Freeman and himself.

Freeman suddenly gets an idea about what Peterio is saying "Oh! " He sighs. Then he points at himself and indicated through a hand signal that he wants to see the space vehicle!

The three step outside and walk to the meadow, where they left the space vehicle safely parked. Their communication with the Galileans is established, and it is in the English language that Galileans and Humans converse in. As their vocabularies are not complete with all the words they needed for a talk, the Galileans sometimes make gestures with their hands.

Peterio pulls Andreus aside as Freeman inspects the intricately but beautifully built space vehicle. It is a model built for space travel at high speeds, by several engineers from the Planet JFK69 at Milky Way, specialized for Peterio and Andreus. It was constructed to handle warp speed and the frequent travel through wormholes that Peterio and Andreus has to do.

"Do you think he knows where we came from. With those pictures I showed him, I can see he got the message that we came from elsewhere. And we got here by space vehicle. He must have figured something out, as he wanted to come here to the space vehicle. But I revealed to him that we are all related. These inhabitants may know that there were different things on Earth that they may have remembered. Different scenery and different wildlife. Then, maybe not! These ones here could be descendants of the pioneers who arrived here. Could they have come in a different manner that is not very apparent? But they must have communicated somehow, about their old home and their new home. We must have added to their ideas, by coming here. I'll show him the pictures of the wildlife from the pictures of the past on Earth." says Peterio who is invigorated to take on this task.

Andreus remarks, *"Why don't we also show him some more pictures illustrating some of the history of man on Planet Earth?"*

116

Peterio says to Freeman as the two head back to the space vehicle "*Do you like our space craft?*" Freeman says as much, waving a finger at the space vehicle. "*I like your spacecraft and I like you!*" His face glowing, he laughed out loud.

Peterio comments, before they all leave the meadow, "*Good! I have more pictures to show you! Let's get back to the huts.*"

All three go back into the hut and seat themselves around the table. Peterio finds the pictures on his computer file and scrolls through numerous pictures which feature events from a time different and prior to their current time, in the history of mankind. It is seen on Freeman's face that he is overwhelmed and perplexed. Some of the comments made by Peterio is in understandable language to this Galilean. Perhaps there is plenty on his mind regarding his new knowledge; that he just is speechless, sitting with the two visitors, smiling. So Peterio decides to give a gesture to have some lunch and call it a day till Freeman can digest all his new information.

The next evening, Freeman arranges for a big outdoors feast party to welcome Peterio and Andreus, and also celebrate the good news that more children have been born since their last visit. Freeman shouts out for the children to parade around the table where Peterio and Andreus are seated. Peterio and Andreus reach out and grab some of the children to give them a hug. All the children crowd around Peterio and Andreus for the huddle. They all laugh. Freeman tells them to get back to their seats, and the children all run off. Freeman who is overjoyed, makes a gesture of the space vehicle, and nodding to the visitors says, *"They came to visit us here from the skies, by space craft."* Upon this remark, all are beaming in enthusiasm and feel a sense of comradeship with Peterio and Andreus. They enjoyed Freeman's feast and all of them stayed outdoors into the evening to chat and also sing for the two visitors."

One evening, Peterio unpacked the space vehicle of more small gadgets that the two brought back from Earth and the colonist planets. These items built at the colonies are gadgets that the natives can use in their daily lives but they are built for the technologically advanced. Peterio will have to deliver some necessary instructions.

Peterio remarks "*In the morning, I will show Freeman what we brought this time for them.*"

Andreus remarks, "*Well, we did wait to see if they would build the steam engine, use coalfire, or develop electric gadgets, use electricity. It took over 300 years in duration for those inventions to surface on Earth. It's a bit demanding to expect a similar scene, an age of inventions, here. And we have really only been visiting less than a century. So, I hope they like our gifts.*"

Peterio notices, "*When we harnessed electric energy with the wind and water turbines for them, they started to use electricity for gadgets that were built in the colonies. They are very happy with that.*"

Andreus agrees, "*They adapted to the technology fast. As also when we brought in some space age gadgets for them to use. With our help, they learned how to use these computerized tools.*

Peterio remarks, "*We can see that Galileans will be for now, non-techie, but with our intervention can become techie. Most of the gadgets I brought this time is wireless and need only to be charged by solar panels. After this visit, we shall see if they prefer our technology. Hey! They are learning arithmetic,* language, and grammar with our computers and calculators!"

Andreus wonders, "*These fancy gadgets will make life easier for them and get them started on something! Maybe! They may one day make gadgets of their own?*

The Galileans are all impressed and joyful as they were presented with new gadgets to use. They know Peterio and Andreus are helping them to change their lifestyles. These gadgets which run on electricity are like toys to children and were met with excitement each time that Peterio brought in more. The new gadgets capture their attention and for hours they would fiddle and examine their electric instruments and tools, adjusting the switches on and off. Their big dream is that one day as Peterio and Andreus continue to help them, they will get on board the space vehicles and go beyond also.

Peterio says to Andreus while they were alone, "*Do you think we need to go to the future to see how things turn out here? We can convince the Force that the Galileans have already accepted us, on friendly terms. These people show intelligence and capability. At Earth, I said they evolved from being hunter gatherer to village farmers. They may adapt much more because all around them the space age is here with them.*"

Andreus agrees, "*We can see that they have the potential to adapt. We have exposed them to new technology in a forward manner by thousands of years. Also, they have now the computer which will be convenient for their communication with us.*"

Peterio says, "*Why don't we bring this back to the Committee?*" Andreus gives *a thumbs up.* "*OK! Let's do that!*" agreed Peterio. "*In the meantime, I want to give Freeman a ride around the planet.* "

Andreus replies, "*We have room for at least three or four passengers*".

On that note the two went to see Freeman about the travel plans.

The Committee decides not to teleport anyone to the future of the Galileans. They also have accepted that this Space Age technology for the Galileans must be agreeable to Force. He must have planned for these primitive people, as they were on the road to be civilized, to make a fast forward change, to adapt to the Space Age. All felt that Force had intentionally navigated Peterio and his crew to Galileo. Probably Force had something in mind, but with good judgement. He allowed both the space farers and the planetarians a chance to make their own decisions. "*In this Galaxy all planetarians found of Earth or non-Earth origins, are planet bound. We came with our Space Age technology and these Galileans expressed interest to be like us.*" reminds Peterio in agreement with the Committee.

Andreus agrees with all the anthropologists and says, *"We have a good relationship now with the Galileans. We can arrange events with them and not need to go to the future. We will just debate on the justification for all plans of action with the Galileans and move ahead with it. The Galileans are demonstrating genuine interests for all that we brought for them! They will develop further with the influence from Force and us space explorers."*

Peterio loves a good story and sees the potential good about to unfold in this historical event. "*They are our long-lost brothers. Although, we are separated by a vast distance in Age, in the development of the Human Race. It is nonetheless a union of Sapiens, Space Age meets Primitive! Definitely, we honour the Force for having connected our Human family, all over the Universe's space-time continuum.*"

Chapter 9 - Extra Earth Communication

Many years had passed, and many spacefarers of the Committee of the Planetary Anthropologists reconvenes back on Earth to debate the Ancients and the Archaic Humans, and the planets on which they live in the galaxies, the Andromeda and the Triangulum. Amongst Earth scientists, the spacefaring members of the Earth Space Agency gather today at Earth Space City. It was indicated to Ambrose Watson that a task enquiry into the intellectual capacity of all planetarians of the Milky Way, the Andromeda (M31), and the Triangulum (M33), for interplanetary communication and for extra Earth radio communication is now needed. This important task meeting will include Peterio, Andreus, Alfred, Gisellin and Evala among the other space farers, astronomers and scientists, as well as government officials. Tedrid, a first Denisovan to be at such a meeting is greeted by all.

Peterio indicated *"The Galileans now ride with us in our space vehicles and have Space Age gadgets. Our colonist engineers set them up with instruments which run on electricity brought to them from wind and water turbines, and solar panels."*

The board discussed the potential of these Galileans at Triangulum (M33) to adopt the technology completely. A government official asked if they are able to start building the same or new gadgets for themselves. He says, *"When they are ready to build, engineers from the colonies will educate them."*

"As with everything," Peterio says *"they will go at their own pace. We will stand by with great anticipation and look out for the day when they can build structures for astronauts to travel into space and structures for astronomers to send and detect radio astronomical signals from both other advanced civilizations and other astronomical bodies. On Earth the Heavens were viewed by eyesight, then by telescopes, thousands of years before technology started and advanced us to where we are today. If they take up our technology they actually will be advancing through thousands of years!"*

All the guests had topics to discuss, and the chair of the meeting allowed them all to have their opportunity to speak. Since the debates, the Board was most interested in discussing the Archaic and Ancient Humans. The conversation stayed on the primitives, but it switched from a talk of the Sapiens at Galileo to those Archaics on planets at Andromeda. It was acknowledged that they have no space technology of their own and are supplied by the colonists. They love the Space Age that they were introduced to. Their fascination with space flight is rewarded when they participate as passengers in the interplanetary flights. However, only the Denisovans progressed in science, outside of the Sapiens species. The Denisovans are studying with the colonists and some are scientists with the Project: Interplanetary Travels at Denisovana. The Denisovans are semi-capable technologically. They learned to use space gadgets while they are passengers on the flights. They themselves, have not developed any space engineering. In actuality, the Denisovans have led the way for the Neanderthals, possibly for some Archaics newly discovered, the Heidelbergensis, and the Erectus, to be included in an enhancement in lifestyle. Alfred and Tedrid had thought that all these species have made great strides in their involvement with the Space Age. They were glad that the colonists had made this pivotal decision to include some of them in the spaceflights. After these highlights have been made in the discussion, Peterio introduces the presence of Tedrid. Peterio wanted to point out that Tedrid is the director of the Project of Interplanetary flights at Denisovana.

Alfred says *"For now, all of them are just happy passengers with the Colonists. Perhaps Tedrid can advance to the level of pilot and make us all proud. And soon!"* He says this jokingly, knowing Tedrid is swamped with paper work at the present.

Alfred and Peterio debated with Tedrid whether all these races of Humans can start developing the technology to send and detect radio astronomical signals. Peterio adds *"The Denisovans developed some engineering technology of their own. The space technology may interest them as they all have love of space science, especially everything that has to do with space flights. But the science involved in astronomy and astrophysics may only be useful for them, in the Project, and those who are involved, such as you, Tedrid and your assistants. Generally, the Denisovans have studied science, but they are not exposed to all that the colonists are used to."*

Ambrose wanted to say that for all the Earth originated planetarians, their Age in Human development, is very different from that of the Space Age Homo sapiens sapiens. That he says will determine the span of time needed for their education into the Space Age. *"On the path to the Space Age, there were many points where the branching had led to all sorts of new activities. Some of these Earth born activities may be bypassed for these humans out here. But we definitely should talk about those various technological advancements in communication and transportation."* says Ambrose. He agrees with all the

Board that it is going to be an exciting development to watch, as all these populations are mostly isolated from each other, living in their own planets.

The chair seeing that Alfred waved his hand, signalling his interests to talk, gave him the go ahead. Alfred wanted to talk also about an assessment on species development. He noticed that the scientists amongst them like Peterio have had generations of academics and scientists in their family history, giving them genetic predisposition to technology and science learning. He says that Tedrid is a first-generation scientist who, along with assistants, are amongst non scientifically directed Denisovans. Although Tedrid, who was Alfred's student, has not advanced to the level of Peterio nor himself. Alfred believes that Tedrid is improving the capabilities of his Denisovan assistants, for learning science. Evala remarks that Tedrid will pass on his genetic predisposition for learning science to his descendents. That started Tedrid to smile at all the comments directed at him and the Denisovan people. Everyone clapped for him.

Evala finds this an interesting topic and continues to remark on the genealogy of the colonists and the Galileans. She reminds the Board that the colonists have some gene mixing of Sapiens with the Neanderthals and the Denisovans. The Archaics at Andromeda are all pure and have no Sapiens in their blood. Also, the Galileans were a population of Sapiens who were relocated to Galileo from Earth and had not met Neanderthals nor Denisovans. Evala says *"I am really fascinated and will study the genetic traits or the phenotypes of these newly discovered Humans. I plan to travel to their planets at Andromeda and to Galileo for this."* Everyone clapped for Evala.

Back to their discussion of radio astronomy, Peterio wants to know if any of the colonists have any signals from their work in radio astronomy. Have the astronomers advanced further than himself in seeking out advanced civilizations? They have signals from the Archaics and Ancients probably because they were given gadgets that signal in the detectable spectrum of wavelengths. Peterio questions *"But have you any signals from any of the searches for intelligent life beyond these Archaic Human colonies? As there was an alien visitor to Denisovana, it may be that signals from our colonies may have been detected!"*

Ambrose questioned why there was an intelligent visiting species who landed at Denisovana for a friendly visit and without much ado left in a hurry.

Without any serious contact with either the Denisovans or Sapiens there, they left. No one knows where they went or if they should come back to Denisovana. He wonders if such a visit will occur at the planets where dwell the other Archaics or colonists, or elsewhere at Andromeda. *"What could be the reason for a single visit from an outsider?"* questioned Peterio.

Suddenly their talk wandered to a consideration on warfare between any visiting intelligent life and any of the forms of the Human race. They talked about weaponry that was developed on Earth and on some other planets at Milky Way. None of the newly discovered Humans know about the weapons development, as they mostly were preoccupied in their adjustments to their own particular lives, and their visits with the colonists. So far, all these Humans, whether Archaic, Ancient, or Space Age live peacefully in their newly found way of life. There had been only this one visit from an outside space farer, that they know of. The brief visit was also friendly. Any encounter with aliens in warfare is not wanted. All these newly discovered Humans are ill-equipped and not prepared for technologically advanced warfare. However, it is the intention to remain on guard for the protection of all these Humans, now.

Gisellin suggested *"I can take the data from the 600 years of space exploration and planet colonization and run a computerized simulation of planetary growth and development for the next 500 years to help all these Humans. I will get it started at Zenos with the supercomputers soon."* For now, he is taking notes on the highlights of the Agenda which included radio astronomy for their new goals. Everyone agreed and clapped for Gisellin.

Andreus wanted to speak on the extra Earth species at Triangulum (M33). He knows that upon observation he suspected at least one of the planets housed an intelligent species. Peterio and Andreus have not had time to study thoroughly from space nor make trips to organize land studies. He suggests *"Next to the discovery of the Galileans, this planet will be an important study for us and I foresee that Peterio and I will be out to visit Triangulum more frequently."* They need more time at the planet to see if Andreus is right.

Peterio informs the group at the meeting that both he and Andreus are looking forward to more explorations with Force. In the search for other intelligent life forms, they feel a need and are compelled to visit with the colonist astronomers. The space in the Universe where the Humans have explored and settled has not been found as places where other intelligent life inhabit.

Beyond is open territory and is where Peterio and Andreus envision, a discovery of intelligent life, foreign to Earth life. All the guests at this meeting believes in their ultimate, preeminent finding of an alien species with advanced technology. From Earth and the colonies, the ESA and other former space agencies had arranged the sending of a multitude of signals or spacecrafts that carried messages from the Earth since the 20th Century AD, in the hope that other extra Earth intelligence will discover that Earth has intelligent life on it. They all believe that their vested interests in "contacting with other intelligence" will produce results, and it will be just "around the corner" when it happens as they indulge in more space explorations.

The possibility of interplanetary communication in the form of radio astronomy signalling for the Ancients and the Archaics became a new idea the Board decided to look into. They acknowledged that all the newly discovered planetarians are becoming techno-logically oriented and education into different techniques of astronomy could be an agenda item for further talks. The study of advanced astronomy followed an intricate path, and the group had decided that all the differing colonies of Humans can be involved in different aspects of a large-scale astronomy project in outer space.

After this exciting talk with each other, the enthusiastic Board made an effort to close the meeting. The agenda for their future work was so interesting to debate, that they all are happy to leave Earth again, to pioneer in their newly organized missions.

The End

References and Further Reading

Films:

Decoding Neanderthals. NOVA (2013) WGBH Educational Foundation.

First Peoples. Their story is our story. (2015) Wall to Wall Media Ltd. PBS Distribution

Great Human Odyssey. PBS (2015) Clearwater Documentary Inc. (2016) WGBH Educational Foundation. (2016) PBS Distribution

Secrets of the Dead. Caveman Cold Case (2013) Terra Mater Fractal Studios GmbH

Picture Books:

DK Featuring New Images from NASA from Earth to the Edge of the Universe (2010) Dorling Kindersley Limited, DK Publishing New York NY USA

Imaging Space and Time Hubble. Devorkin, D& Smith R.W. (2008) Smithsonian National Air and Space Museum in association with National Geographic Society. Kessler, E Chapter 5

Books: (Nonfiction)

A History of Communications (Media and Society from the Evolution of Speech to the Internet) (2011). Poe. M.T., Cambridge University Press.

Brief History of the Mind (2005) Calvin, W. H., Oxford University Press.

Darwin and Design (2004) Ruse, M., Harvard University Press.

Gaia: A New Look at Life on Earth (1979), reprint (1995) Lovelock,J., Oxford University Press

Lone Survivors. How We Came to be the Only Humans on Earth (2013) Stringer, C., St. Martins Griffen. Macmillan Publisher

The Medea Hypothesis Is Life on Earth Ultimately Self-Destructive? (2015) Ward P., Princeton University Press.

Books: (Fiction)
Hominids Neanderthal Parallax #1. (2003) Sawyer. R.J., Tor Books.

Articles:

The Evolution of Modern Human Brain Shape (2018) (Jan 24) (4:1). Neubauer, S., Hublin,J.J., Gunz, P., Science Advances.

What Does It Mean to Have Neanderthal or Denisovan DNA. (2019) (May 14) Genetics Home Reference http:ghr.nlm.nih.gov/primer/ dtcgenetictestingneanderthaldna.

We may have Lived with Denisovans Much More Recently than We Thought (2019) (April 1) Wilson ,C., New Scientist.

https://en.wikipedia.org/wiki/ Interbreeding between archaic and modern humans

https://www. nasa.gov
https://www.jpl.nasa.gov

CPSIA information can be obtained
at www.ICGtesting.com
Printed in the USA
BVHW041818220620
PP10887900001B/1

9 781999 181406